Fake Dating the Grumpy Bigshot

A Sweet Romantic Comedy

Book 4

Too Busy for Love series

By Leah J. Busboom

Published by LBRB Consulting, LLC
First edition 2023
Published in the United States of America

Dedication

To all of you who enjoy romantic comedies, may this story make you laugh out loud.

To my amazing husband—I couldn't do this without your love and support.

I don't know how people can fake whole relationships . . . I can't even fake a hello to somebody I don't like!

—Unknown

Prologue – Enemies Forever....................................7

One – The Ultimatum 18

Two – The Dog Park...22

Three – The Light Bulb Goes On 27

Four – History Majors Need Not Apply...................33

Five – Laverne and Shirley 39

Six – The Agreement..49

Seven – The New Assistant 54

Eight – Glimpses of the Sweet Boy Next Door 57

Nine – The Dating Disaster 62

Ten – The Fake Dating Scheme 69

Eleven – Fake Dating Rules 73

Twelve – Crullers 80

Thirteen – Signing the Star Pitcher........................88

Fourteen – Is it Couture?..92

Fifteen – Cinderella at the Ball..............................97

Sixteen – The Charming Mr. Bigshot 103

Seventeen – The Debacle Part 1 113

Eighteen – The Debacle Part 2 125

Nineteen – Where Do We Go from Here?..............133

5

Twenty – Between a Rock and a Hard Place..........*136*

Twenty-One – You Got What You Asked For..........*139*

Twenty-Two – Breaking Another Rule...................*142*

Twenty-Three – A New Rule and An Epiphany.......*146*

Twenty-Four – Meet the Mastersons *150*

Twenty-Five – Bumping into an Old Friend...........*162*

Twenty-Six – History Majors Please Apply.............*168*

Twenty-Seven – Handing Over the Team *177*

Twenty-Eight – Landing the Dream Job................*180*

Twenty-Nine – I'm an Idiot! *187*

Thirty – The Blue Dress *191*

Epilogue – Love You Forever *199*

Note to Readers...*205*

Acknowledgements *206*

About the Author...*207*

Prologue – Enemies Forever

Libby

A Year Ago

I'm taking in a baseball game today with my brother Griff and his girlfriend Arielle. Personally, I'm dreading the outing because Mr. Bigshot will be here. But Griff begged me to come.

Griff is still on the team's injured list after his shoulder surgery a few months ago. My brother was an All-Star on the team until the tear in his shoulder, so the team wants his presence at the final game of the season. An appearance to show that Griff's on the road to recovery and give the fans hope that he's coming back next season, although that isn't a given. A local game announcer is going to briefly interview him during the seventh inning stretch.

Spirits are high because the team has already secured a spot in the playoffs, so I was looking forward to attending the game. When the invitation came to sit in the owner's box, I almost backed out. But knowing Griff's morale needs this recognition, I reluctantly agreed to attend—after a lot of arm twisting by both Griff and Arielle.

"The owner's box is fancy," Arielle whispers behind her hand as we walk into the luxury suite. Since I've never been to an owner's box before (lowly sisters don't usually rate these invites), I tend to agree. But I'd expect nothing less from Mr. Bigshot. The guy is always "on" and always trying to impress. Sometimes I wonder what's genuine and what's fake with him.

Griff chuckles at his girlfriend's wide-eyed look while she takes in the over-the-top furnishings in this ritzy private party room. Across one wall is a serving area with granite counters and a fully stocked bar. None of the lavish snacks set out on the countertops are your typical ballpark fare.

Waist-high café tables surrounded by shiny barstools are scattered throughout the air-conditioned suite so guests can eat and drink while watching the game. There's also an outdoor sitting area for us commoners who are used to watching the game from the stands. The digs are certainly extravagant.

I'll just ignore my sworn enemy.

Brent Masterson, aka Mr. Bigshot, is the team owner's son and heir to the throne. We became next door neighbors when I was in fourth grade. Griff and Brent were sixth graders at the time and quickly became best friends. I was the tagalong little sister they tried, usually with great success, to ditch.

During my sophomore year in high school, Brent started noticing me. I'd been attracted to him since middle school (and unfortunately he's only gotten hotter since), but he never noticed me then. When he asked me to prom, it was like a dream come true—until it wasn't.

What was supposed to be a magical evening became a nightmare when Brent stood me up. And being the immature high schooler that I was, I did my best to avoid Brent from that day on. I spent the rest of high school embarrassed and hurt over "The Debacle," as it came to be known. And Brent never once tried to make things right. Needless to say, we've been sworn enemies ever since.

I scan the room nervously, looking for Mr. Bigshot, hoping to keep as much distance as possible between us. He's schmoozing with a distinguished-looking man in a suit and a woman wearing diamonds. Lots of them. My heart does a little flip because Brent looks like a million bucks in his suit. It fits him like a glove.

Griff is enthusiastically greeted by team personnel. They wave him over to some comfortable couches on the other side of the room.

"Do you want to talk about me being on baseball's injured list?" Griff asks Ari and me with a grimace.

"Nope. You go ahead. Libby and I will hang out together," Ari says. He kisses her on her cheek, leaving us to fend for ourselves.

Several tables are already occupied by people wearing clothing that look couture—the women are clad in dresses you would wear to a high-end restaurant, the opera, or a charity gala. The men are in expensive-looking suits and polished shoes.

Oops! My jeans, T-shirt, and baseball cap are definitely out of place.

"I think we're a bit underdressed," I whisper to Arielle. "Wish someone had told us the dress code."

She giggles. "At least we'll be comfortable, unlike the rest of them."

Her lack of concern over our faux paus surprises me. But I remind myself that we aren't here to impress anyone, we're here to watch the game.

As I tear my gaze away from the A-listers, Brent's eyes lock with mine. His previous sucking-up-to-the-wealthy-guy look is replaced by a scowl. I feel like sticking my tongue out at him, but my adult side refrains. Instead, I tug my companion to the snack and bar area located at the opposite side of the room from where Mr. Bigshot is standing. "Let's get some of this fancy food and drink."

We peruse the snacks—lavish hors d'oeuvres made from mysterious ingredients and presented on silver platters. No pretzels, popcorn, or hot dogs to be found. You're apparently supposed to eat these things on cocktail napkins, because there are no plates in the suite, paper or otherwise. Since Ari is a party planner, she oohs and aahs over the food, while I wish I could get a hot dog slathered in mustard and a diet Coke.

A cute bartender engages us in conversation as we place our drink orders. He's several years younger than me, but that doesn't stop me from flirting.

"I'd love a diet Coke, please," I say, batting my eyelashes at him. Out of the corner of my eye, I watch as Brent's scowl deepens.

Cute Boy grins. "Are you sure you don't want something a bit stronger? How about a rum and Coke?"

"She just wants a diet Coke," a familiar crabby voice says. I jump, and the young bartender flushes then scurries off to retrieve my beverage from an under-the-counter fridge at the other end of the bar.

My turn to scowl at Brent. "How do you know I don't want something with a little more kick?" I put my hands on my hips and huff at the grumpy intruder. He's standing about a foot away and smells so good—like fresh air and sandalwood—I want to put my nose against his neck and sniff.

Get a grip, Libby!

Brent's eyes narrow. "We both know you'd fall flat on your pretty derrière after one drink."

My lips purse and my neck heats, although I admit his acknowledgment of my attractive backside makes my stomach flip.

Is he remembering that *one time* when I came home from college, just barely twenty-one, where I tried a beer at a neighborhood picnic? After drinking less than half the can (I'm a lightweight, I know), I became so tipsy Grams had to ask Griff and Brent to escort me home. Turns out they both had to hold me upright and practically carry my woozy self the two blocks to our house. If I remember correctly I did some loud, off-key singing and may have asked Brent to marry me.

The bartender shoves my canned beverage in my hand before I can make a clever retort to Brent. I settle for giving Mr. Bigshot a frosty stink-eye as I sip my diet Coke. He glares at me like he just sucked on a lemon.

Ari pops up between us. "Brent, this spread is so nice!" She's clearly trying to thaw the ice between Brent and me. "Who's your caterer?"

The two of them chat about party planning details while I grab a few of what looks like tiny meatballs, plus something resembling pigs in a blanket—I choose those because maybe they'll satisfy my craving for a ballpark hot dog, although I'd have to consume twenty of them since they're so miniscule.

Carefully balancing the food on the undersized napkin—which is a feat considering I chose round food—I reluctantly rejoin Ari and Brent, who've moved several steps away and have sat down at a nearby café table. I re-scan the room, wishing they had plates rather than just these microscopic napkins. I guess it keeps guests from chowing down on the food.

After I manage to scramble onto the high barstool—which was a feat while keeping the meatballs from rolling off the napkin—I bite into one of the tiny morsels and my mouth instantly turns into a nuclear blaze. *Goodness! What's in these meatballs?*

I cough, then chug my diet Coke, hoping no one will notice the sweat forming on my brow. Grams would reprimand me over my unladylike guzzling of the beverage. Adding insult to injury, my nose also starts to run. Thankfully I grabbed a couple extra napkins so I can discreetly dab my leaky nostrils.

A pat on the back tells me I haven't been discreet. "Are you okay?" Ari asks. Brent smirks at my discomfort—he knows full well that my lack of tolerance for spicy food rivals my lack of tolerance for alcohol. He's probably remembering that time Griff and he enticed me to eat tacos they'd slathered with hot sauce. I had a similar response to their evil trick.

"Yep, I'm fine. It's just a little spicy," I croak.

After getting my leaky nose back under control and soothing my burnt throat, I feel the need to leap into the conversation between Ari and Brent as a distraction from my spice blunder. The topic of discussion has moved on to baseball and whether the team has a strong chance for a deep run into the playoffs. Ari's knowledge and ability to rattle off stats makes me feel like a third wheel, so naturally I add my two cents worth. "Boy, the team's OPS numbers are really in the tank. Maybe they should focus more on batting practice," I spout out, directing the comment to Mr. Bigshot, while having no idea what an OPS number is. Despite my brother being a pro baseball player, I've never gravitated to the stats side of the game. Plus they keep adding new ones, so who can keep track?

He quirks an eyebrow. Ari clears her throat. "Actually, the team has the best OPS percentage in the league," she whispers.

Well, so much for showing off my baseball knowledge.

"Um, well, there's always room for improvement," I add in a breezy voice.

"Looks like you're dressed for a baseball game," Brent says, his tone implying that I'm not dressed appropriately.

"We're *at* a baseball game," I fire back.

"Touché," Brent replies. I think he almost wanted to smile at that one.

"Looks like you're dressed for the office," I say, then snap my fingers and add, "Oh, right, I forgot, this is your office." I suppress a wince. My tone sounds overly condescending, even to my own ears.

Ari, who's sitting to my left, turns and gives me a stern look. If she was my mother she'd be saying, "Behave yourself!" There's just something about Brent that brings out my surly nature. He rubs me the wrong way, like an ill-fitting shoe.

"Libby, how's the job search coming? Grams mentioned you're still looking," Brent says, in what would sound to an outside observer like a politely interested tone, as he sticks the knife in and twists it. My inability to land a job in my degreed profession is a sore spot, and he just knowingly stepped into a minefield.

Glaring across the table, I say, "I'm being very particular and don't want to settle."

Translation: I'm still unemployed.

His face morphs for a few seconds into surprise, then returns to a grumpy scowl. *Did he really not know?*

"She's hot on the trail of several positions," Ari pipes in, trying to smooth things over.

Translation: I've applied for fifty-two jobs just this week.

"Yeah, I'm sure to land something very soon!" I say cheerily.

Translation: A blind squirrel occasionally gets an acorn.

An awkward silence falls over the table.

Ari's look of consternation makes me feel guilty, so I grapple for a safer topic. "It looks like a wonderful day for a baseball game," I say brightly, falling back on the weather as a neutral conversation starter.

Just as the words leave my mouth, a loud thunderclap echoes around the stadium. Players and fans scramble for shelter as the rain comes down in sheets. The PA announcer says the obvious when he declares, "Folks, we're in a rain delay."

So much for talking about the weather.

Swiping one of the pigs in a blanket from the cocktail napkin in front of me, I take a bite, hoping to fill my mouth so I can't say anything else stupid. My nose wrinkles and I almost gag when an acidic taste hits my tongue. I desperately want to spit the offensive food into my napkin, but with Brent and Ari sitting here, I can't do that without them noticing.

Ugh!

13

I chew as fast as I can, trying to rid my mouth of the horrible taste. I probably look like an overzealous chipmunk. When Brent stops a waiter and takes one of the horrible-tasting bites from the serving tray, I try to subtly shake my head to warn him. These things are so bad, I wouldn't wish them on my worst enemy. *Oh right, he* is *my worst enemy!* Brent ignores my head gesture and pops one of the appetizers in his mouth.

In seconds, he scrunches up his face, then spits the bite into his napkin, obviously not shy to do so in our presence. He sucks down almost a full bottle of water while Ari and I watch.

"Why didn't you warn me?" he rasps, his voice sounds like a sick bullfrog. His eyes drill into mine as if I made the horrible tasting food.

"Why me? I didn't make those awful things," I grumble.

"You just ate one," Brent points out. "Your enthusiastic chewing was the reason I took one."

A snicker slips out. "Enthusiastic chewing? That was me trying to choke the blasted thing down."

We glare at each other while Ari looks on with both interest and humor. "I'm going to catch up with Griff and leave you two to your, er, discussion." She nods her head towards the side of the room where Griff is standing, then waltzes away. *She abandons me now?*

With our buffer gone, Brent and I might come to blows. I take a deep breath, trying to calm myself.

"What is in those things?" Brent wheezes, still chugging water like a man who spent the last week in a desert.

I tentatively pick up the one remaining pig on my napkin and sniff it. My eyes water and my nose crinkles. Whatever is in these things it smells like a combination between smelly feet and burnt toast.

14

Another waiter flits past, so I put out a restraining hand to stop him. "Can you tell me what's in these? Mr. Masterson thinks he chipped a tooth. Are there any olives with pits in these, by chance?" I say, nodding towards Brent. "Can you check on the full list of ingredients as well? I'm wondering what's giving these such a, um, er, distinct aroma." I quickly rephrased from what I wanted to say, which was *horrendous smell*.

The waiter's eyes widen in concern while Brent's glower deepens, annoyed at my little white lie about his chipped tooth.

"Oh dear! Mr. Masterson, my sincere apologies! Are you in pain?" the waiter says in a voice that carries across the room— probably a wannabe actor, with that vocal projection. He wrings his hands while I bite my lip, trying to suppress my laughter. The guy could win an Academy Award with his performance.

Several pairs of eyes swivel to stare at the agonized waiter, Brent, and me. If Brent were a cartoon character, steam would be blowing out his ears, plus his face has turned a shade of red that matches his tie.

"I'm fine," Brent mutters.

"He's had quite a bit of dental work, crowns and even a false tooth, so you can understand the cause for concern," I add in a low voice.

The waiter stares at Brent's mouth as if trying to discern the extent of his dental work. "Let me check with the chef!" The waiter flees from the suite, the polished wood door slamming shut with a loud bang behind him. Whatever eyes weren't turned our direction before are staring at us now.

I maintain a pleasant smile on my face, trying to look nonchalant while sipping on my drink. Brent plasters on a fake grin and waves a dismissive hand. "Libby thinks she might be getting hives," Brent says to the room, while mimicking scratching his forearm. "She was inquiring about ingredients in the appetizers. Better safe than sorry!"

Murmurs of concern float across the room. One lady puts her hand up to her lips, giving me an O-shaped sympathetic look.

I kick Brent under the table.

"Ow! What was that for?" he says, rubbing his shin.

"For blaming me as the cause of the ruckus by the waiter," I say in a low voice, smiling like a hyena to hide my annoyance.

"You were the one who caused the ruckus!" Brent says through clenched teeth.

Dang! He has me there.

We glare at each other for several long beats, during which time the room returns to normal conversation. Out of the side of my eye, I see Griff and Ari still staring at us with amused, albeit somewhat embarrassed, expressions on their faces. I should probably try to hide my disdain for Brent a little better. But I do so love jabbing at him.

Brent and I maintain a stony silence until the breathless waiter returns. "There are no olives in any of the appetizers. The chef mentioned that the Vieux-Boulogne cheese in the pigs in a blanket has a distinct pungency, giving it zest and piquancy."

A politically correct way to say the cheese smells like a dead mouse.

I put my hand across my heart. "No pits! Thank goodness! What a relief!" Turning to Brent, I say, "Mr. Masterson, maybe you chipped your tooth earlier when you were sipping on that martini? The one with the large olive in the glass." I give Brent a gentle nudge from my foot under the table, hoping he'll play along.

"Yes, that's probably what happened. I grabbed the olive out of the glass when you swiped the martini from my hand." Brent rotates to addresses the waiter. "She can be a little aggressive when it comes to drinks involving vodka," he says with a wink.

I feign a delighted giggle. "You're such a kidder, Mr. Masterson."

The waiter looks from Brent to me and back again, as if trying to figure out whether one or both of us are crazy. Uncertain what to say or do next, he bows and excuses himself, disappearing back out the door.

"Well, you scared him away," Brent says.

"I believe it was all your dental work that perplexed him," I shoot back.

Griff appears at our side and gives me a disapproving big brother look. "The rain has stopped, and they've resumed play. Shall we go watch the game?"

Ignoring Brent, I leap to my feet. "Yes, that sounds fun."

Ari slips in beside me as we stroll the twenty-eight steps to the outside seating area—I count them as we walk, trying to get my annoyance at Mr. Bigshot under control. "I thought you two were going to come to blows. What happened?" she says after we sit down.

Griff makes sure that he and Brent are on Ari's other side, as far away from me as possible.

"He's infuriating," I say, my jaw clenching. Griff says something to Ari, and she turns to chat with him and Brent, giving me a chance to ponder what just transpired.

Brent and I mix like the proverbial oil and water. If he says black, I say white. He says yes, I say no. We literally rub each other the wrong way. It's better if we aren't in the same room together. *Thank goodness our one date never went anywhere.*

With Griff's return to baseball questionable, maybe I won't have to cross paths with the infuriating Mr. Bigshot in the future. I can only hope.

One – The Ultimatum

Brent

Present Day

Today's request to come to Dad's office isn't out of the ordinary. He's been giving me more and more responsibility in the organization, cumulating in naming me Manager of Player Personnel a few months ago.

Dad is slowly loosening his grip on the professional baseball team empire he's owned and managed for over thirty-five years. It's been his life. However, the constant stress of keeping the baseball organization profitable has taken a toll on Dad's health. Mom's been promoting the concept of retirement for a while, and it's just a matter of time before Dad succumbs.

Wonder what's on the agenda today? Dad seemed rather tight-lipped on the phone.

"Come on in, son," he says when I arrive.

"Dad," I say as we exchange man hugs. The kind where we hug rather awkwardly and give each other back slaps. Hugs with Dad are always like this; the only person who's invested in real hugs is Mom.

"Sit. I've got some coffee brewing. Do you want a cup?" He nods towards the battle-scarred coffeemaker at the back of the room. It's one of those clunky Mr. Coffee makers that Joe DiMaggio used to hock in the seventies and eighties—in the iconic, gaudy harvest gold color, no less. The commercials were long before my time, but Dad's mentioned on several occasions that he bought the machine solely based on the player's endorsement. We've even got another functioning one in the executive conference room. Hey, at least the machine is durable and long-lasting.

"I'll pass," I reply, having already consumed a tall half-caff Americano with a splash of soy milk before I got here. I might be a little finicky in my coffee choices.

Dad shrugs and takes a seat behind his massive desk as I sit in one of the uncomfortable guest chairs. An oversized coffee mug, two pencils, and a pad of paper occupy the desk along with a clunky computer monitor. Dad needs an upgrade on all his electronics. But in a few years, I guess all he'll be worried about is whether he owns the latest TaylorMade driver.

He takes a slurp of coffee while I shift in my chair. "Your mom says it's time for me to retire. Hand the reins over to you. Six months from today it'll be a done deal," Dad says without further ado.

My jaw drops. "Are you ok? You're not sick, are you?"

He waves his hand. "No, other than my usual high blood pressure, I'm fine. It's just time to move to a place in Phoenix and hone my golf game," he says with a grin.

"But . . ." I reply, at a loss for words. I thought this announcement was still months, if not years, away.

Dad chuckles. "Brent, I've been grooming you to take over. You're ready."

I slump back in my chair. *Am I ready to take over?* A boulder that I didn't feel prior to entering the office settles on my shoulders.

Tapping a pencil idly on the desk, Dad's eyes bore into mine. "There's just one thing."

"One thing?" I repeat like a robot.

He sighs. "Your mom and I are worried that you haven't settled down yet. You date women you have no interest in. Like that model you took to the charity gala? If the wind blew, she'd catch her death of cold."

I cringe. He's right. My last date—whatever her name was—had the skimpiest dress I'd ever seen. A scarf has more fabric. Not that I complained.

The pencil tapping increases as he carefully considers his next words. *Tap tap. Tap tap. Tap tap.* "You've got six months to get engaged. Find someone you can settle down with. Otherwise, I'm going to sell the team."

"What!?" I almost leap from my chair. Shifting to a stiff upright posture, I glare at Dad. *Has he lost his mind?*

His eyes narrow. "You heard me. This deadline will be good for you. No more frivolous dating. You've always done better when there's a clear goal in mind."

"Did Mom put you up to this?" I huff. She's always trying to get me to date a daughter of one of her friends or a niece of her hairdresser.

"Your mother and I agree on this subject."

Tap tap. Tap tap. Tap tap.

"Dad, you know you can't predict when you'll find 'the one.' If you hadn't bumped into Mom in that elevator, you'd have never met her."

The irritating tapping stops and he grins. "That was fortunate." Memories about how he met Mom obviously play in his head as he nods and smiles. A few seconds later, his expression morphs to a more serious one, and he says, "However you find 'the one,' do it."

"But it's not that easy." My voice sounds a little whiny, even to me.

Dad scoffs. "It isn't easy if you assume every first date with someone is already the last one with them. You go through women like water through a sieve. What was the name of the last woman you dated?"

I squirm in my chair. "Um, Astor?" *Or was it Aspen? I get definite Colorado vibes now that I think about her.*

"You don't remember, do you?" Dad says, a look of concern etched on his weathered face. *When did he get so old?* His computer pings and his eyes swivel to the bulky screen. "My next meeting will be here in five minutes," he says and stands.

I feel like I'm being dismissed from the principal's office.

"Mom and I look forward to meeting your future wife. Soon."

As I walk down the hall towards my own office, my mind swirls with who I know that's even a candidate for the future Mrs. Masterson. It's a short list. Actually, it's an empty list.

Libby pops into my head. *Why on earth would I think about her?* Of course the only attractive single woman I know is the one woman who hates me as much as she hates oysters. She'd rather eat a hundred hot-sauce-covered tacos than spend more than five minutes with me. Of course, she probably thinks the same about me—though the truth is I've never gotten over my high school crush. When I'm around her I try to hide my real feelings for her behind a shield of arrogance and grumpiness since I know she hates me. It's becoming more and more difficult to separate my fake feelings for her from my genuine ones.

But if not Libby, then who?

Two – The Dog Park

Libby

When I adopted my new puppy at my grandparents' fiftieth anniversary party, I was a tad worried about the daily commitment of taking a dog on a walk. I'm sort of a nonexercise girl. Yoga pants are to be worn sitting on the couch and not at a class that requires you to twist your body into a pretzel.

The heaviest weight I lift is my coffee cup every morning. Let me tell you, by the fifth cup, my right arm has had a great workout. Don't even mention cardio activities unless you mean sprinting to the fridge for the last scoop of Rocky Road Fudge ice cream.

The notion of walking any distance *every single day* with my new pooch was a rather daunting thought. It even crossed my mind to acquire a used treadmill—obviously not for me—so my furry friend could use it. My retired baseball player brother called me out on how lazy the treadmill idea was and pointed out that, in fact, my health would also benefit from daily walks.

So, here I am on the daily walk to the dog park, my sweet puppy strolling beside me, sniffing every fire hydrant, bush, and tree on the way. *What is the attraction to smelling those things?* I admit I took a small sniff at her favorite bush one time and ended up with a nose full of pollen. Don't sniff a fully blooming azalea.

Our round trip walk to the dog park is a perfect 1.8 miles. I know this because I drove my car the distance in order to be able to brag to my brother about my new exercise routine. His reaction was to snort and tell me to find a dog park further away from my apartment. *Fat chance.*

When we arrive, a handful of other owners and their dogs are frolicking at the park. The dogs, not the owners. The dogs are romping around off leash in a gated area while the owners sit on the benches provided for our use. I spot the only empty bench, let my puppy off her leash, and sit down, relieved to have a few nonexercise minutes to read the news on my phone.

Though the glare from the bright California sun does make that a little difficult. The cap I'm wearing is pulled low and sunglasses hide my eyes. It probably looks like I'm trying to hide in plain sight, but I'm not. Before Griff retired he had to wear disguises like this in public because one can never be too careful of lurking paparazzi.

Now that my brother Griff isn't a celebrity any longer, he rarely appears in any of the news feeds. But his annoying friend recently made the news and I've been reluctantly/eagerly following the story.

It's called curiosity, ok?

Brent Masterson—aka Mr. Grumpy Bigshot—was recently named to replace his father as the manager of the baseball team my brother used to play for. The Bigshot was my brother's best friend once upon a time, thus my obligation to keep abreast of news regarding him. *That's what I'm telling myself.*

My eyes are glued to my phone reading a gossip rag article about Brent. He looks hunky in a perfectly tailored business suit while the woman on his arm is wearing a miniscule dress. I'm not actually sure that it qualifies as a dress.

I look up occasionally to make sure Wilma is having a good romp. She's the sweetest dog and I don't know how I got along without her. Needless to say, the walks are worth it.

"Is this seat taken?" a familiar male voice asks.

I jump and look up. My jaw drops because none other than Mr. Grumpy Bigshot is standing beside my bench.

"Libby! I didn't expect to see you here," Brent says, as he awkwardly waits for my response, looking like he's debating between sitting or fleeing. "Um, I can find another bench."

"No need. Please join me." The polite invitation slips out of my lips without my permission. I internally kick myself and want to suck the words back in. His unexpected appearance didn't give me time to activate the usual defenses I use to resist him. Prickliness. Aloofness. A touch of disdain.

Brent's surprised expression is quickly replaced by a frown, something I've termed as Resting Grump Face—his usual expression around me. I've seen him smile, and it transforms his handsome face, making my knees go weak and my heart rate kick up a notch or two. Thankfully he's not using that expression right now. Grouchy scowls I can deal with, hunky smiles I cannot.

He grudgingly settles on the bench beside me like I have a disease he doesn't want to catch. I know his mom is big on manners, so he's probably only perching out of a sense of politeness. Giving him a side-eye glance, my heart does a little flip when I see what he's wearing. Pressed khaki shorts that hug his butt, a tight-fitting T-shirt that shows off a well-developed set of pecs, and a backwards baseball cap completes the ensemble.

My slouchy shorts and ratty T-shirt have seen better days. Wasn't there a hole under my armpit? Suddenly self-conscious, I keep my arms pinned down at my sides. I may have just rolled out of bed and come here. *Why didn't I at least comb my hair?*

An awkward silence hangs between us. I rack my brain for a topic of conversation that won't bring us to blows. Commenting on the weather (my usual fallback conversation topic) seems like a safe, albeit boring, topic. I certainly don't want to stick my foot in my mouth again by commenting on baseball stats, if I knew any.

As I open my mouth to comment on the blue skies overhead, Brent thankfully cuts me off. "Look, Fred is playing with your puppy," Brent says, nodding his head towards the pair happily frolicking with each other, unlike their owners who are barely tolerating each other. Brent also adopted his puppy at my grandparent's party, and they're siblings. In fact, they look remarkably alike.

"Her name is Wilma," I say.

Brent shifts on the bench to face me. "As in Wilma Flintstone?"

I nod and a blush travels up my neck. Brent, Griff, and I were big fans of watching *The Flintstones* when we were kids. A recent *Flintstones* binge inspired me.

Didn't he say his puppy is named Fred?

I arch an eyebrow. "What about Fred? How did you come up with that name?"

He looks a little embarrassed, as his Resting Grump Face turns red. "Um, well, I might have named him after the cartoon character."

I laugh. "Are you still watching reruns?"

He grimaces. "Maybe?"

Oddly, our mutual fondness of *The Flintstones* helps break the chill between us. We smile tentatively at each other—which we haven't done in years—both finding amusement in the coincidence. "It looks like Fred and Wilma are getting along well. How often do you come here?"

"I try to come as often as I can, but my assistant walks him when I travel with the team."

He has an assistant? Of course he does. He's Mr. Bigshot. For a moment I'd forgotten that he's a bigshot. I was thinking of him simply as Brent—my brother's best friend, the boy next door, and my post-prom-debacle enemy.

I nod. "It's been a real breakthrough for me to adhere to an exercise schedule, but I come every day."

Knowing my aversion to any activity that requires movement or sweat, he grins over at the parking lot. "Which car is yours?" he asks with a teasing smirk.

I elbow him in the ribs just like I used to do when he and Griff would tease me. "I'll have you know, Mr. Masterson, that Wilma and I walk all the way here from my apartment, rain or shine."

That's a fairly easy boast when you live in a part of the state with an average 283 days of sunshine. No wonder California is so overcrowded.

Chuckling, Brent says, "Do you always come here around this time?"

"Yep, I'm a working gal, so I gotta get my steps in before eight," I joke.

His smirk broadens when I mention steps. Whoever came up with that crazy ten thousand steps every single day rule probably never walked a thousand steps a day in their life. I'm perfectly content with my five thousand, thank you.

"Maybe Fred and I will see you sometimes," he says.

Huh? He actually wants to see me again? My brows draw together, and I frown, emulating his Resting Grump Face. Thoughts about the prom debacle flood into my brain, spoiling the moment. He needs to explain that situation before I let him back into my life. Maybe even do some groveling that involves ice cream.

As if he reads my mind about groveling—or maybe it's the fact that my scowl looks like I accidentally ate an oyster (I hate those slimy things)—Brent makes a show of looking at the watch on his wrist, then hops to his feet. "I've got a meeting in forty-two minutes, so I need to get going. Nice to see you again Libby." He calls for Fred and flees as if his pants are on fire.

"Well, Mr. Bigshot, you're going to have to do a lot of begging, pleading, and explaining if you hope to make friends with me again," I mutter to his attractive retreating backside. My brain tries to remind me he's my enemy, but the truth is, my heart finds him irresistible. *Too bad he hates me as much as I act like I hate him.*

Three – The Light Bulb Goes On

Brent

When I get to the office, I hide behind closed doors—the meeting excuse being just that, an excuse. I mull over seeing Libby at the dog park and cringe at how I let slip that Fred and I might bump into her and Wilma again. While my voice displayed excitement at the possibility, she looked like someone who was told they needed dental work.

My family moved next door to Griff and Libby's grandparents when I was in sixth grade. Griff quickly became my best friend. His athletic prowess inspired me to join Little League with him— something no amount of cajoling by my dad had ever convinced me to do. By the time we were in high school, I also ran track and played basketball, Griff being the star in those sports and me merely participating.

Libby was the annoying little sister, always trying to tag along with Griff and me. We tolerated her presence sometimes—like when we wanted her to snag some chocolate chip cookies from the kitchen—but mostly tried to ditch her, often leaving her in tears.

She wasn't allowed in the treehouse because we declared it a "boys only" zone. We erected a rope ladder that we'd pull up whenever we climbed inside, leaving her stranded on the ground. If we had popsicles, we grudgingly shared the flavors we didn't like with her. One summer her lips were permanently tinged lime green. When riding bikes, we peddled faster than her, our longer legs leaving her discouraged and in the dust so she'd give up the chase and tearfully ride back home.

I cringe. Looking back, I can't believe we treated her so poorly. Twelve-year-old boys don't worry about hurting a girl's feelings.

It wasn't until my senior year in high school that I realized how pretty Libby is. My attitude towards her went from annoyance to attraction. I finally screwed up my courage and asked her to prom. I'll never forget how her eyes lit up when I asked. Was it merely because I was a senior asking a lowly sophomore to the dance or was she interested in me? By the excited look on her face, I choose to believe that she was genuinely interested in me.

Of course, an unfortunate prom night incident—caused by my mom and Grandma Laverne—ended any romantic relationship before it could get started. Libby believed I stood her up and when Griff took me to task, I stubbornly dug my heels in and refused to offer any explanation. She went back to being the annoying little sister, only worse, and from then on we've acted like enemies rather than friends.

Knock! Knock!

Dad opens the door a crack and peers in my office as I scramble to look busy by moving my mouse and staring intently at the blank screen. After a few clicks on the keyboard, I glance up and say, "Hey, Dad. What do you need?"

He plops down in a chair across from my desk and blows out a loud breath. For the first time, it hits me how exhausted he looks. Every wrinkle and gray hair suddenly stand out, and my heart lurches. *Dad is an old man.* No wonder he doesn't want to run this organization anymore. "Sam Hudson wants to be traded. His agent just informed us that he's not going to accept our new contract offer."

I scowl. This is terrible news. First we lose Griff the All-Star hitter to injury, and now we're going to potentially lose our star starting pitcher.

Sam is the reason we fill seats at the ballpark and were able to make a run deep into the playoffs last year. I thought we were close to signing his contract extension. The fact that his agent did an end run around me, as Manager of Player Personnel, to inform my dad about the request makes my blood boil. If I were a cartoon character, fire would be shooting from my eyes.

"I'm on it. Let me handle this," I say in a terse voice, not even trying to hide my annoyance.

"You know we can't afford to lose him. I thought we made him our best and final offer. Can we relook at the figures?"

I nod, my mind already spinning with how to restructure some other contracts to make room in the budget to give Sam a higher offer. "I'll work up a new number right away and review with you."

Dad nods. "Thanks, son. I'll be glad when we get this one buttoned up." He stands and treads out of my office, every step painfully measured like he has concrete in his shoes. His shoulders are more stooped than I've ever noticed before. *Is Dad hiding something about his health?*

My heart beats faster; I need to step up to the plate and take the reins of this organization as soon as possible. Dad's ultimatum plays in my head. It doesn't seem possible to find a woman I'm interested in enough to date seriously—rather than my usual no-strings-attached approach—let alone get engaged to in six months. My short list of potential dating candidates is embarrassingly short.

Click!

Urgency makes a light bulb turn on in my brain. Could I possibly persuade Libby to *fake* date me? Fake dating someone would solve all my problems—still no strings attached, but fulfilling my parents' wish. And Libby's one of the few women I'd feel comfortable about fake dating. There'd be zero risk that she'd fall for me. There's more risk that a cow would fall from the sky. Outside of a tornado, when would that ever happen?

All we'd have to do is convince Mom and Dad that we're serious. Libby is a pretty good actress. Assuming I can be as convincing as her, in a few months Dad will hand over the organization to me, Mom and he will move to Arizona, and afterwards Libby and I will break up. If I'm honest with Libby upfront, we can each go our separate ways with no messy feelings, no broken hearts.

But how do I get her to agree? Right now we barely tolerate each other, although we bonded over Wilma and Fred and actually spoke more than two words to each other at the dog park. That's a start. I'll probably have to do a lot of begging and pleading—possibly involving ice cream or me being her indentured servant for life. At least that feels more possible than actually finding someone I want to marry in just six months.

Relieved that I've got the beginnings of a plan figured out for this fake dating, fake fiancée thing, I boot my computer and get to work. We can't afford to lose another star player.

~*~

No more than ten minutes later, my assistant Penny sticks her head in the door. "Got a minute?"

I sigh at the interruption, but Penny is too loyal to toss out like I'd do anyone else. I try to keep my grumpiness in check around Penny because she handles all my requests efficiently and without complaint. "Sure," I say after saving the spreadsheet I'm working on.

She plops down in the chair across from my desk, a beaming smile on her face, and she extends her left hand forward. "I got engaged!" she squeals, wiggling her fingers back and forth, the diamond on her ring finger sparkling in the office fluorescent lighting.

"Congratulations!" I say, trying to enthuse positivity into my voice. Penny and her boyfriend have been dating for several months, but I didn't know they were this serious. I get a bad feeling in my gut that this isn't going to be good news for me. Plastering a fake smile on my face, I wait for the other shoe to drop.

"Luke got a great job in Bakersfield. We're going to be moving there in two weeks," Penny says. Her smile slips. "I'm sorry for the short notice, but you need to find a new assistant as soon as possible so I can train him or her." She folds her hands in her lap, looking genuinely contrite.

The other shoe drops with a thud.

I sit up straighter in my chair as urgency regarding the short timeline smacks me in the chest. Penny has been such a terrific assistant; I hate to lose her. At the same time, I'm not going to stand in the way of true love. Suppressing my frown, I say, "Well, then, can you write up a job posting, and we'll start the search immediately?"

"Certainly!" she says, jumping back to her feet. "Thanks, boss!"

She's gone in a waft of strawberries, which I find a little overpowering but have come to accept. Libby smells like vanilla and cinnamon, as if she just baked cookies and the aroma clings to her skin in a subtly pleasing way.

Why am I thinking about how Libby smells?

Glaring back at the spreadsheet, I return to structuring a new offer for Sam. I feel like a magician trying to pull a rabbit from his hat since the team finances are so tight.

Click!

Another light bulb turns on. Libby, who's as smart and resourceful as Penny, would be an excellent assistant. But this morning she mentioned that she's already got a job. Could I persuade her to come work for me instead? With our rocky history? The fact that we treat each other more like enemies than friends? At least with fake dating she could still hate me most of the time. Working together, on the other hand, would require us to be civil most of the time.

31

Still, I'm holding on to that slight glimmer of hope, based on our interaction at the park where we didn't come to blows—figuratively, not literally, of course. And the more I think about it, the more it seems like a job offer would be an easier first sell than fake dating. If there's one thing my current job has trained me to do, it's put together compelling job packages.

You know, maybe this is exactly what I need. Real assistant first, fake girlfriend later. That might even make the story more believable with my parents. I feel a smile crawl slowly across my face. *This could actually work.*

I resolve to present Libby the most convincing job offer I've ever made the next time I see her, which hopefully is tomorrow morning at the dog park. Get her to agree to that, then feel her out on the fake dating plan. As Mom always says, it doesn't hurt to ask—or in this case beg, grovel, and plead. Desperate times call for desperate measures, and I can be very persuasive.

Four – History Majors Need Not Apply

Libby

"It was only a little fib," I say to Wilma as we stroll into my tiny two-bedroom apartment. She cocks a spotted ear but doesn't comment further. I'm feeling a tinge guilty about my "working gal" comment to Brent because it was basically a big fat lie.

"Are you back from your *big* walk, amiga?" my roommate calls from the kitchen, the Spanish endearment rolling off her tongue. She's never met a stranger and terms of affection are second nature to her. During a traffic stop for speeding, she even called a policeman amiga. Maybe that was to convince him to give her a warning instead of a ticket?

My roomie appears, still in her Grumpy Cat festooned PJ's, clutching an oversized mug of coffee. Her naturally curly brunette hair (which I'm jealous of) is piled haphazardly on her head. Even dressed in sloppy clothes and without makeup, she's gorgeous. Her curves and snapping brown eyes attract men like flies to honey. I, on the other hand, blend into the background like nondescript wallpaper.

Wilma scampers over, gets a pat on the head, then trots off to the kitchen where I hear the sounds of lapping water. The noise reminds me that I really need to get a rubber mat to put under the dog bowls.

"Would you like a cup before starting your exhausting job search today?" She extends the mug and gives me a commiserating pat on the back, then disappears back into the kitchen for her own cup. We both require at least two cups of caffeine before we can function.

Margarite Consuelo DiSilva Coronado is a force of nature. Because her name is quite a mouthful (although it rolls musically off her tongue), she insists we call her Maggie. She's employed by some top-echelon architecture firm in the city which allows her to set her own hours, and work mostly from the comfy confines of our apartment.

As you can tell, I'm not only jealous of her hair, but I'm also jealous of her career, especially in light of my present job—or lack thereof. But her sweet and caring nature instantly wins you over. There's not a harsh bone in her body. She's like a jolly grandmother, understanding bestie, and astute career advisor rolled into one.

She joins me as I plop down on the tiny couch, which really only qualifies as a love seat. The apartment doesn't have room to fit any full-sized furniture. Griff always teases me that I live in a dollhouse. With my currently strained finances, I can't afford a bigger place. Griff has said he would happily help me out. But I don't want to be a leech, and I love this cozy apartment and rooming with Maggie.

"Anything exciting at the dog park? Did Wilma have another run-in with the Great Dane?"

The "run-in" as Maggie calls it consisted of Wilma barking at the Great Dane and scaring him into fleeing back to his none-too-happy owner. My puppy has the moxie of an Irish Wolfhound despite her petite size.

"No, not that. But we did bump into someone." My brows knit together at the conundrum churning inside me at seeing Brent.

Maggie reaches over and smooths my brow with a fingertip. "No frowns, amiga. You don't want to get wrinkles." The woman has perfect skin. She's dedicated to daily sunscreen applications, resists frowning or scowling, and adheres to a nightly regimen of pricey products that guarantee a youthful appearance. With my meager salary, I can barely afford those budget lotions sold in large twenty-ounce bottles at Target. "Who did you bump into that caused such an unhappy face?"

34

"Griff's friend, Brent. He grew up beside us. I think I've mentioned him a couple times."

She nods knowingly. "Ah, yes, the guy from the prom debacle story."

I sigh. "Yep, that's him." *Maybe I tell that story too often.*

She giggles. "From the look on your pretty face, I suspect that he's more of a dilemma than you're letting on. You're not sure whether he's a friend or an enemy. And maybe you want him to be more?" Sipping her coffee, her brown eyes bore into mine, waiting for me to confess the truth.

The seconds tick by as I squirm in my seat, then take several more sips of the hot beverage. As another delay tactic, I point out the window. "Blue skies, and no clouds in sight." Why I always comment on the weather when I'm nervous, I don't know.

Maggie arches a perfectly manicured eyebrow, not letting me off the hook.

"Oh, alright! I admit that I might be a tad bit attracted to him." I fold like a bad poker player. In fact, Gramps told me one time that my poker face sucks.

A grin splits my roomie's face. "Better yet! Will you be bumping into him again?"

"Maybe," I grumble. "He adopted one of Wilma's siblings."

Maggie's delighted laugh floats around the room. "Oh, this is so good! We need to improve your walking attire. Add a little spice to your athletic wardrobe." Her fingers make a drumbeat on her mug as she rattles through all the apparel catalogs stored in her head. The woman is a fashionista, and she's on top of all the latest clothing trends. She'd give Kate Hudson and Carrie Underwood a run for their money.

I glance down at my worn shorts and sloppy T-shirt and cringe. My wardrobe needs a facelift—the depressing truth is I need new exercise clothing that isn't a castoff from my older brother. I could use some of those cute tanks and figure-hugging leggings in bright colors, possibly even a matching jacket.

Before I get too carried away, my lack of funds slaps me in the face. *Womp! Womp!* With my current salary, I'm lucky to afford ramen noodles and pay the rent. Having zero frivolous spending money is going to severely hamper being able to afford any snazzy outfits.

"Well, this is all I can afford until I find a real job. Plus, I'm not interested in having a boyfriend."

Maggie snorts. "Okay, whatever you say my friend. But I bet you and Brent start dating before the end of the month."

My eyes widen at her bold statement. "What makes you think that?"

"You've never admitted to being 'a tad bit attracted' to anyone before. It's just a matter of time. And how convenient that you both have puppies that need walking!" She claps her hands in glee, pats my knee, and heads down the hall. "I've got a Zoom call in fifteen. Adios for now," she throws over her shoulder.

I drag myself to my room, change into my fuzzy pink bunny slippers, and slouch down in front of my computer, ready for another frustrating day of applying for jobs and being rejected. Wilma lounges at my feet, oblivious to the fact that her owner is barely able to afford dog food. I need to find a real job—one where you comb your hair, slather on some lip gloss, and wear big girl clothes—as soon as possible.

The grandparents and Griff warned me that it would be difficult to find employment in my chosen field of study. I scoffed at their warnings, blindly moving ahead, and obtained a B. A. in American history, with a minor in art history. I found the topic fascinating and thought I could get a job at a local art museum as a curator, educator, or archivist.

I didn't consider the small number of art museums in the California area where I reside, or the fact that apparently the people they employ are there for life, so there's very few, if any, job openings. I've widened my search beyond California even though I don't want to move, but the only jobs I've found have been twelve hundred miles away, making them nonstarters.

Jiggling my mouse, I search the major job boards, hoping to find something, anything, I can apply for. I've resisted venturing too far out of my field up to now—especially since I do have a source of income, no matter how crummy it is. Maybe, after months of searching, I should quit holding out for a job that will use my education. Would a company want an executive assistant who's well versed in American history? Let's see what I can find.

~*~

Three o'clock rolls around, I shrug my shoulders and rub my weary eyes. After scanning all the major job boards for hours, I've applied for one measly job, and it was a stretch in terms of fit. Nonetheless, I crafted a witty cover letter advocating how an American history degree could be beneficial for a librarian assistant position.

Only forty-five minutes to get ready and bustle off to my current odious job. Snapping my laptop closed, I shuffle my suddenly weighed-down feet to the closet and pull out the dreaded uniform.

At first the waitress job at Harv's Diner wasn't too bad, other than the hideous uniform we're required to wear. The employees are all older than me, but most of them are friendly. For the most part the diner patrons are nice older people on limited budgets.

While I enjoy serving the geriatric set, very few of those who frequent the diner are decent tippers. I suspect it has to do with the fact that the diner attracts only the extremely frugal customer, one looking for a cheap meal. They all seem to think that a ten percent tip is overly generous, and many leave far less than that. One time a lady left me a quarter beside her plate.

I tug on the hated dress and cringe when I look in the mirror. Ruffles and bows dominate the ugly brown uniform. The skirt is too short, the bodice too frilly, and the poofy sleeves remind me of swimming floaties. It's an unattractive combination between what the UPS man and a Stepford wife might wear.

Buckle up, buttercup!

That little pep talk is one of Gramps' favorite sayings. The waitress job is only temporary—and necessary to pay the bills— until I can find a dream job in my chosen career. At this rate I'll be serving up blue plate specials until I'm sixty.

I grab my thrift-store acquired designer purse—amazing how astronomically the price of these goes down when they're the previous year's fashion. Wilma gives me her sad puppy dog look, knowing I'm leaving her.

"Go keep Maggie company," I command, and Wilma trots off down the hall, yipping and wagging her tail.

"You don't have to be that excited about it," I mutter, knowing full well that everyone, including my sweet puppy, can't resist my roommate's charms.

"Come in, sweet Wilma!" Maggie says with delight, then her door snicks closed.

Okay, time to earn some money. I square my shoulders and head out, wondering what unfortunate incidents await me at Harv's Diner tonight. Sid's working the cook line and whenever Sid's in charge, things don't go well.

Five – Laverne and Shirley

Brent

This isn't how I imagined I would be spending my Friday night. But here I am.

When Mom called to ask if I would accompany (read: pick up, pay for meal, and return home safely) Grandma Laverne and her sister Shirley, my initial reaction was to decline. However, because I've been haggling with Sam Hudson's agent all week, I needed a break from fretting over our star pitcher's contract. So I relented, figuring the outing would be, at a minimum, interesting.

When I arrive at the designated time, the two women are waiting on the front porch, looking every inch the Southern belles that they are.

Grandma was born in a small town in the South where the iced tea is sweet, the men are genteel, and ladies' clothes are frilly. She dresses up to go to the grocery store, so you can imagine what she's wearing for this outing.

Her pink flowery dress's delicate material flows as she walks, covering her modestly from chin to six inches below the knee–all the lace and frills would look gaudy on anyone else, but look right on Grandma. Her low-heel black patent shoes are both sturdy and stylish. She carries a matching black patent pocketbook (her terminology, not mine) and an umbrella, although I don't know the last time we had an unexpected rainstorm here. Great-Aunt Shirley is similarly attired, but her dress is lime green. I blink when the sunlight glints off it, wishing I had my sunglasses.

"Brent, dear boy, thank you for taking us to dinner!" Grandma says as she approaches my Audi SQ7. I assist first her and then Shirley into the back seat. They always insist that they ride behind me, as if I'm their chauffeur. *Maybe I should invest in white gloves and a black cap?*

"Ooh! This is quite the luxurious vehicle. Is it new?" Grandma asks as she smooths her hand along the rich leather seats.

Our conversations always start off the same way, inquiring about my car, then moving on to asking about girlfriends, and lastly about whether I've "put on a few pounds" since we last saw each other. Despite being eighty-eight years old, my grandmother is predictable—though still sharp as a tack.

"I bought it last year after we won the division championship. It was kind of a thank you from Dad."

"And what is the price of something like this?" Shirley asks, wrinkling her nose at the extravagant expenditure.

A quiet *gasp!* comes from the other backseat occupant. "Shirley, dear, no asking about money! Brent, please forgive my sister and her deplorable manners."

The two squabble in low voices while I back out the driveway, trying to suppress my laughter. It always strikes me as ironic that they have the same names as the quirky pair on the TV sitcom since they were named long before that television show ever aired. They could give those two a run for their money. Snippets of their conversation drift to the front seat.

"Proper ladies don't ask rude questions—"

"Young folks want you to ask so they can brag—"

"It's unbecoming behavior—"

"Laverne, you know I'm a dyed-in-the-wool woman's liber—"

"Mama would roll over in her grave. Now hush."

A glance in the rearview mirror shows both back seat occupants fuming after their little dustup. Shirley has her arms crossed, a mulish expression on her face. Laverne's inspecting her nails as if they are the most interesting thing in the world. The silence won't last long.

Three . . . Two . . . One . . .

"How's your love life? Any nice girls caught your fancy?" Grandma pipes up. "Your mother says that you're starting to date more seriously, with an eye towards settling down."

I glower, the ultimatum from Dad echoing in my head. "Um, well, that's an optimistic outlook seeing that I'm not currently dating anyone."

"It's okay to be particular," Shirley adds. "You should take as much time as you need, dear."

Not when you have a deadline of six months ticking like a time bomb over your head. "I agree, Aunt Shirley," I say, glad that not everyone subscribes to Dad's, and apparently also Mom's, crazy demand with an unrealistic and unreasonable timeline.

"But don't take too long. You'll be an old man before you know it," Grandma says. "Aren't you approaching thirty?"

This coming from an almost-ninety-year-old?

I resist the urge to laugh. Thankfully we arrive at the diner and both ladies drop this line of conversation in favor of debating what the blue plate special is going to be.

~*~

We're seated in a booth near the back of the diner by a dour-looking older woman. Thankfully I've escaped dining at this establishment until now. Mom usually accompanies the elderly pair, and I was only called into service because of a last-minute meeting for Mom's volunteer group at church.

I take in the ambiance, or lack of it. The place is worn down from the scuffed linoleum floors to the water-stained popcorn ceiling. The fake red leather benches in the booths sport cracks all over, and most of the barstools at the front counter lean to the left. Harv's Diner is stuck in the fifties, but not in a fun, quirky, vintage way. Most of the workforce looks to all be over fifty, and their mud-colored uniforms are the ugliest ones I've ever been unfortunate enough to set eyes on.

Laverne and Shirley debate the menu and merits of various dishes, while I try to suppress my frown as I hide behind the oversized menu—which is as big as a posterboard—hoping no one I know notices me. I need to keep up my suave businessman persona, and Harv's Diner doesn't jive with that image. *Impress to be impressive.* Although chances are slim that any of my circle of friends would come here.

"The meatloaf comes with a side of those glazed carrots. I just love those things," Shirley says.

"But the chicken-fried steak includes a biscuit rather than one of those plain dinner rolls. I think you can even ask for two."

Laverne's suggestion makes Shirley's eyes light up like a Christmas tree. "I'll ask about substitutions when the waitress arrives."

She's been here a hundred times and asking about substitutions just occurred to her?

I groan internally as my frown deepens. A conversation about substitutions will take no less than five minutes, maybe ten. The ladies will then dawdle over their dinners, delicately cutting their meat into tiny pieces, slowly sipping their sweet tea, maybe even asking for more rolls. Our dinner outing suddenly stretches to well over two hours, and that might be cutting it if they decide to have dessert. I peek over to the dessert case, which shows no fewer than five different types of pie, along with what might be cheesecake.

I won't be home until after nine.

"Good evening, ladies. Welcome back to Harv's Diner. May I take your beverage orders?"

I nearly drop the menu at the sound of the familiar female voice. "Libby?" My frenemy works *here?* Based on her working gal comment at the dog park, I thought she had a nine-to-five office job.

Her eyes fly to mine, and a dark red blush stains her cheeks. "Brent. I didn't notice you with the menu hiding your face."

At least my hiding-in-plain-sight-plan is working. Or was.

Libby is clad in one of those atrocious uniforms, though despite how much the sight burns my retinas, the short hemline shows off her legs nicely. I can't help but stare.

Grandma chuckles. "My grandson can be a little shy around the ladies."

Libby grins while a blush now heats my face. Leave it to my grandma to be embarrassingly blunt.

"I was reading the vast menu choices," I say in a huff, flapping the menu still clasped in my hand. It creates a draft that lifts Aunt Shirley's bangs.

My octogenarian companions exchange a look. Libby arches an eyebrow and taps her pen on the tiny pad clasped in her hand. No one is buying my lame excuse.

"Beverages?" Libby prompts.

Both ladies order iced tea—sweetened, of course—and I order a Coke. My frown tips into a half smile since the beverage order goes so smoothly. *Maybe they've forgotten about the earlier substitution discussion?*

"And are you ready to place your entrée orders?" Libby asks, politely nodding towards the ladies to go first.

"Are substitutions allowed, dear?" Shirley says. *Nope. Here we go . . .* Not waiting for a response, Shirley plows on. "I want the meatloaf plate, but with two biscuits. Those plain dinner rolls simply aren't filling enough."

Libby nods. "Yes, we can make that substitution. Do you still want the side of carrots?"

"What are the other choices?" Shirley asks.

43

My frown returns in force as I slouch down in my seat, wanting to bang my head on the tabletop. The person who declared she loves the carrots is now asking about other choices?

"You can substitute the creamed corn," Libby replies.

"Oh no, that won't do!" Laverne chimes in, shaking her gray head, though not a single hair moves because of all the hairspray she's applied. "You know how corn comes out looking the same as it did going in."

I wince at the image that statement brings to mind. Libby's lips twitch, but she doesn't comment.

"Okay, I'll have the meatloaf plate with the side of carrots and two biscuits," Shirley confirms. "Can you include five pats of butter, dear?"

"Of course," Libby says, not at all put off by the request for the odd number. My brain spins, refusing to ignore the fact that Shirley ordered five pats of butter for two biscuits. *Does that mean she's going to use two and a half pats on each biscuit? Or possibly two pats on one biscuit and three on the other?*

"I'll have the chicken fried steak, but with the side of carrots and not the green beans. Beans give me gas. Oh, and I'll also have two biscuits," Laverne says as Libby scratches on the little pad, her face not reacting to the gas comment, while I want to crawl under the table.

"Brent?" Libby prompts, her eyes twinkle as they meet mine. I think she's enjoying my elderly companions' antics.

"I'll have the hamburger with fries."

"I think you can substitute coleslaw for the fries, dear. A much healthier choice," Grandma says.

Before Libby can open her mouth to confirm the change is allowed, I say rather tersely, "The hamburger and fries, no substitutions."

Laverne and Shirley frown, both looking disappointed at my lack of interest in adding variety to my meal.

"Do you want mustard, ketchup, two pickles, a dab a mayo, and a slice of lettuce?" Libby asks, trying to keep a straight face.

I scowl. "Sure. Whatever toppings are standard is fine."

"I thought you offered sliced fresh tomatoes as a topping," Laverne says.

"Sorry, but we're out of tomatoes," Libby replies.

"Do you have any substitution for the tomatoes?" Shirley pipes in.

"No substitutions!" I thunder in a much-too-loud grump-filled voice. Three pairs of eyes stare at me wide-eyed as an awkward silence falls over the table.

"I really don't need tomatoes," I squeak in a mortified tone, then take a gulp of ice water. Sweat beads on my forehead, my heart rate is accelerated, and I feel like a misbehaving two-year-old.

"Two pickles are kind of a skimpy amount. You'll wish you had more," Shirley adds, oblivious to my agony.

"I'll bring more pickles in a basket in case you decide to live on the wild side," Libby says in a soothing tone, then winks as she disappears back into the kitchen.

"She's lovely, dear. How do you know her?" Grandma asks as soon as Libby is out of sight.

I guess the conversation about my love life, or lack of one, isn't forgotten after all.

~*~

Thankfully I managed to duck the love life discussion by pointing out the carrot cake and key lime pie in the dessert case, which ignited a discussion about the caloric content of those desserts. My cell came in handy for looking up the nutritional information and ending the debate. Carrot cake has decidedly more calories than key lime pie.

We made it through dinner—with Shirley using only four pats of butter—and ordered desserts without any further substitution talk. The ladies were pleased with their entrées, especially the gravy slathered over the mashed potatoes. Shirley raved on and on about that.

My hamburger was average, but edible. I did sneak one of the extra pickles since the patty was so large, and two weren't, in fact, enough. Shirley gave me a thumbs up.

I sip on my decaf coffee while Laverne and Shirley finish their desserts.

"The apple pie is delicious, Brent. I'm surprised you didn't get a piece," Laverne says, holding up a forkful.

"Since you reminded me that I'm getting older, I decided to watch my waistline," I reply with a smirk.

Shirley belts out a belly laugh and gives me a high five at my witty rejoinder.

"There's gravy on my potatoes!" a voice bellows off to our left. "I said gravy only on the chicken and not a drop on the potatoes!"

All eyes swivel to the disturbance, which I admit is even louder than my outburst during the substitution discussion. A burly man glares at Libby, who bites her lip and apologizes profusely. Her face is as red as those tomatoes they were out of.

"I'll get you a new plate right away, sir," she says, grabbing the plate and scurrying back into the kitchen.

"How rude," Shirley mutters.

"Men nowadays have no manners," Laverne adds.

I find Grandma's statement a little off-putting since I'm a man and sitting right here. Due to my recent outburst, though, I don't refute her assertion.

Within a minute, Libby delivers a new plate to the obnoxious man. He scowls down at the offering. "There's hardly any gravy! I want my chicken fully covered," he shouts, shoving the plate back towards Libby. The unexpected plate slides off the table and onto the floor. *Crash!*

The sound of the stoneware cracking rips through the air. The food sits in an unappealing pile on the floor as chicken, mashed potatoes, and gravy combine in a lumpy heap.

A large man wearing a white cook's hat and apron runs out from the kitchen with a mop and a roll of paper towels, then thrusts them at Libby. "Clean up this mess," he says in a sharp tone. He turns to the rude patron and says, "I'll bring you another plate. On the house." After giving Libby another glare, he returns to the kitchen.

Libby mops furiously, looking like she's going to burst into tears. Before I can think things through, I hop to my feet and join her, helping to wipe up the mess with the paper towels. Libby's eyes flit to mine, but she doesn't say a word as we clean together.

The cook delivers the new comped plate, and the man doesn't complain further. Did he make such a fuss just to get a free meal? The surly man picks up his fork and calmly eats, ignoring everything and everyone around him. The other patrons return to their food and discussions. Silverware clanks against plates and conversation drifts around the room, making me feel a little less like a gnat under a microscope.

Once we're done with clean up, I pull Libby aside. "Are you okay?" My heart's beating at a rapid pace; cleanup must have been more strenuous than I thought.

She nods but refuses to make eye contact.

"Hey, don't let them get to you," I say under my breath. "You can't control the amount of gravy."

Her lips twitch for a second, and my heart lifts knowing I made her feel slightly better.

"Will you and Wilma be at the dog park again tomorrow?" The words slip from my mouth before I realize that I desperately want to see her there. I don't even make a flimsy excuse that it's Fred who wants to see Wilma.

Her eyes lift to mine. "Yes."

I nod. "Okay, Fred and I will be there. Same bat time, same bat channel," I say with a smirk.

She squeezes my arm and mouths "thank you" before retreating into the back.

When I slide back in our booth, Laverne and Shirley gawk at me, approval in their eyes.

Shirley fans her face. "How romantic!"

Laverne grins broadly. "Such heroism, chivalry, and gallantry. You just won that girl's heart."

Did I?

Thoughts swirl through my mind. Maybe it won't be as difficult as I thought to convince Libby into the fake dating plan. With how horrible this job appears to be, hiring her as my new assistant looks like a slam dunk. After she works for me for a while, and we don't kill each other, I'll propose the fake dating plan. A two-for-one accomplishment that puts me on the path of taking full ownership of Dad's baseball organization! I justify my somewhat self-promotional plan by telling myself that I'll also be rescuing Libby from this awful job and her having to wear that horrible uniform ever again.

On the downside, will I be able to resist her? That little flaw in my plan gives me pause, but I shove that concern aside.

Six – The Agreement

Libby

I barely sleep, anxious and excited to see Brent again at the dog park. How did he go from being my sworn enemy to something else—dare I say friend—in the blink of an eye?

Events from the diner replay in my head, over and over. The cranky patron . . . The plate of food tossed on the floor . . . Brent diving in to help clean up . . .

A dreamy smile lights my face at how Brent came to my rescue. It was rather romantic how he jumped into action. His quiet presence beside me helped ease the embarrassment and frustration.

My smile turns to a frown, remembering how Sid played a large part in the fiasco. My order ticket clearly indicated no gravy on the potatoes. He never pays attention to details, just slaps the food on the plate and expects us to deliver it promptly and with a smile.

When I returned the first plate to the kitchen, Sid gave me a glare that would scorch wood. He's never liked me, and I'm pretty sure he was stingy with the second round of gravy just for spite.

Why do I work at a place like this?

With very few other employment options, I resolve to do my job at the diner as well as I can. Don't let Sid get to me, keep my chin up, and double check the gravy order before delivering it.

Maybe another employment opportunity will come along soon. A girl can only hope.

~*~

When Wilma and I arrive at the dog park, I'm winded and a bit stressed out. Maggie needed help with a sagging hemline on her business suit. It's the first time she's gone into the office in months, and she was frazzled about looking professional for an important company announcement.

Of course I offered to help! She wouldn't hesitate to help me fix my ruffles and bows on that awful waitress uniform. At least she looked like a million bucks in her suit, whereas I look like an outdated version of a cartoon character. Still, my eyes kept darting to the clock as the stitching process stretched longer than anticipated.

Now my eyes eagerly scan the park. Lots of dog owners are sitting on the benches, their pets playing with each other in the gated section, but Brent is nowhere to be seen. My heart sinks. Maybe he isn't going to show.

Feeling like a foolish teenager again, I turn Wilma loose to play with the other dogs and find an open bench to pout on. *I should have known Brent isn't trustworthy!* The Debacle readily comes to mind, and I berate myself for my naivete as this rant rages inside my head. Even if he shows up, I'm going to give him the cold shoulder.

I try to concentrate on my phone, but my eyes refuse to cooperate as they take an occasional glance—every two seconds—around the park, still hoping that Mr. Bigshot will show up.

What feels like an hour later—but another glance at my phone confirms is only five minutes—my heart goes through another emotional roller coaster as Brent jogs up the path from the parking lot, looking uncharacteristically disheveled. His hair flops onto his forehead as if he hasn't combed it yet today. He's wearing a worn pair of sweatpants and a slouchy sweatshirt, but my treacherous heart still flips at the sight. He turns Fred off his leash and a smile lights my face as Fred makes a beeline for Wilma. Tails wag furiously as the pair greet each other.

"Sorry I'm late," Brent says in a breathless voice as he joins me on the bench. Close up, I see an adorable smear of what looks like grease on his cheek. My cold shoulder quickly melts, and my fingers itch to rub it off.

Arching an eyebrow, I say, "Looks like you had a run-in with motor oil?" Smirking, I point to his right cheek.

He grimaces, swiping at the stain on his cheek but failing to rub it off.

"Here, let me help." Without my permission (or his), my fingers reach over to his cheek and wipe the oil away. Our eyes lock and Brent gives me a curious look.

What's come over me?

Clearing my throat to cover the awkwardness, I say, "Care to spill about what happened?"

A frown crosses his face and the look I know so well—Resting Grump Face—appears. "Don't ask. Let's just say that Grandma Laverne had an emergency with her Lincoln and leave it at that."

Based on knowing Laverne from her previous diner outings—although I never suspected she was Brent's grandmother—I can't help but grin. "Did she want any substitutions when you changed the oil?"

A belly laugh rumbles out of Brent's chest. "She did! There was a long debate at Walmart over motor oil weight and whether to purchase 10W-30, 5W-30, or 5W-40."

Despite the fact I should maintain a cool demeanor (my vow to give him the cold shoulder and all), I join in the laughter. "Well, don't leave me hanging. What weight did you agree on?"

Rolling his eyes, Brent says, "The most expensive one, of course."

I have no idea which oil is most expensive, but I don't pursue that line of discussion any further. A comfortable silence falls between us as we watch Fred and Wilma play.

"I have something I want to talk to you about," Brent says, breaking the silence.

I give a nonchalant shrug, though I'm intrigued. "Okay, I'm not going anywhere."

He shifts uncomfortably on the bench; my heart plummets to my toes. *Uh-oh!* This is where he tells me that meeting like this is a mistake and that he only felt sorry for me when he made the invite last evening. I grit my teeth, waiting for the disappointment to hit.

"Um, I was wondering if you'd like to come work for me? As my assistant."

My jaw drops. *Say what?* I stare at him, wondering whether I heard him correctly. The shy, embarrassed look on his face tells me that it's true that he just offered me a job.

"Really? You want me to work for you? *Why?*"

He winces at my shocked, terse reply, and I wish I could pull the words back and deliver them with more finesse. Especially since my current employment sucks and working for Brent might trump working at the diner, by a gnat's eyebrow.

"Well, my assistant gave her two weeks' notice. I thought, er, um, based on last night's sorry set of events, you might want a new job."

His words make my hackles rise and I wave a dismissive hand. "Hey, I don't need your pity. And I certainly don't need a job offer just because you feel sorry for me."

He reaches over and takes my hand; I resist the urge to yank it out of his grasp. "Libby, I really want you to come work for me. I actually thought of you before I ran into you at the diner. I'm in a bind. You're smart and resourceful. I trust you. I'm sure if we try we can tolerate each other enough to work together." A tentative grin flashes across his lips.

The earnestness of his words soothes the sting of his clumsily worded offer. *Maybe this isn't just a pity offer?* I stare at him, trying to detect an ulterior motive, but only see sincerity and a glint of challenge in his eyes.

Events from last night at the diner come crashing into my mind. I detest working there. Working for Brent can't be any worse; maybe it'll even be better. As long as we don't kill each other. A fresh start might be just what I need. Though I need to make it clear I'm not going to be his errand girl and pick up his dry cleaning.

"Okay. When do you want me to start?"

Seven – The New Assistant

Brent

Unexpected guilt over not telling Libby all the details of my plan haunt me all night. With the clock ticking, I need to make progress towards Dad's ultimatum as soon as possible. And easing Libby into the plan seems like a better option. But is she going to think the job offer was insincere once I reveal the part about fake dating?

Dad strolls into my office on Monday morning, looking dapper in his lime green golf outfit. He and Aunt Shirley would make quite the pair. Since I've taken over the day-to-day operations, Dad's taken on visiting the golf course more frequently—correction, daily.

Squinting, I notice a white tee tucked behind his right ear. Wow, I guess he's serious about his game. Or Mom forgot to tell him he's had that golf accouterment on since yesterday's game. How did it survive the night? *Never mind!*

My eyes move beyond Dad's garish outfit to survey his overall demeanor. Even though it feels like he's abandoned the organization and me, throwing us to the baseball wolves, it's terrific to see him looking happier, healthier, and less stressed. He's a changed man.

"Your mother reminded me of the charity gala next weekend. I assume you and your date will be joining us?" Dad says as he takes a seat across from my desk.

Dang! I didn't think I'd have to persuade Libby to agree to the fake dating scheme this soon.

I almost blurt out "what date?" but think better of it. Mom would just find the daughter of her pastor or a granddaughter of one of her friend's neighbors to go with me.

Instead, I go with a vague reply. "Sounds good."

Dad arches an eyebrow. "So you already have a date lined up? I trust it's not one of those skimpily dressed models you usually take?"

Libby's pretty face floats into my head. She just started today, and Dad hasn't bumped into her yet. Should I drop her name to Dad without cueing her into the fake dating plan first? A resounding *no!* shouts in my head.

Suddenly the flaw in my plan becomes glaringly obvious. Can a guy fall for his assistant enough to invite her to a fancy event—the woman he's been a sworn enemy to for over eight years—in less than ten days? The tight schedule gives me instant heart burn. Maybe I can pawn my newfound attraction to her as a case of *instalove*. After we started working in proximity, we realized our mutual attraction to each other. Blah, blah, blah.

Dad's going to think I'm nuttier than a Snickers bar.

"No, I have someone much more suitable in mind," I say, hoping he takes the hint from my tight-lipped reply that I don't want to elaborate further.

"Brent, I can't find the ding-dang toner for your beast of a printer," Libby says in an annoyed voice, striding into my office, then skidding to a stop. She's become a bit disheveled since earlier, when she arrived looking like a polished executive assistant—thankfully no ruffles or ugly brown material in sight. Her blouse is untucked from her skirt, her hair is coming out of her ponytail, and there's a black smudge on her cheek that my fingers itch to wipe off.

"Mr. Masterson, sir, I'm sorry, I didn't realize you were meeting with Brent." Her face turns beet red, and she looks like she's going to curtsy but thinks better of it.

Dad, the ever-polite gentleman, stands. "Libby Griffin? Well, this is quite the surprise to see you here." He hides his confusion well, knowing Libby's and my history of avoiding each other like the plague.

"I just started today," she murmurs.

"Libby's my new assistant," I blurt as we both talk at the same time.

After an awkward couple beats, Dad chuckles. "Welcome to the team." The look he throws me speaks volumes, as in "I hope you two don't kill each other."

Libby quirks an eyebrow at me, clearly wanting me to take the lead. *I guess I am the boss.* I rack my brain for whether to launch into a long-winded explanation about Libby working at a crummy job—at a diner no less—that requires her to wear the most abominable uniform, and me needing an assistant since Penny's move has left me in the lurch, thus leading to Libby's current employment here. Or whether to bring-up the unseasonably chilly weather.

Womp. Womp.

Maybe awkward silence is the wisest option; I'd just stick my foot in my mouth.

Dad breaks the uneasiness. "Let me get out of your hair so you can locate that toner," Dad says, nodding to the empty cartridge in Libby's hand. "Oh, and son, Mom will follow up with you on the event we talked about. She'll want all the details about your date so we can arrange schedules."

I nod, feeling the walls closing in on me. By *details*, he means the name and social security number of my date, possibly even a photo of the dress she plans to wear. With the charity gala in less than ten days, I've got to come up with a viable date ASAP. My eyes land on the woman standing in front of me. Can I convince her to play along with my fake dating scheme? Probably not in time for the gala.

56

Eight – Glimpses of the Sweet Boy Next Door

Libby

Well, that was awkward.

After Mr. Masterson leaves, Brent and I gape at each other for several more seconds. Our incompatibility is like an elephant in the room. Sworn enemies suddenly working together? Everyone knows our past, including Brent's dad. He probably wondered how we're going to cohabitate in the office without a skirmish. Metaphorically speaking, not literally, of course.

Picking up the forgotten toner cartridge, I say, "Show me where you keep more of these."

A professional expression slips back onto Brent's face. "Follow me to the supply room."

~*~

Day two on the job, and Penny's a no show again for training. I twiddle my thumbs for the first thirty minutes but then decide to leap in with both feet. *I've got this.*

Wandering into Brent's office, I ask, "Do you need me to make travel arrangements since you'll be joining the team on Thursday, rather than traveling out with them on Wednesday night?" I overheard a discussion with Brent and the marketing lady earlier, and I figure as his assistant I should schedule his travel. *A little self-initiative with the boss never hurt either.*

He looks up at me with surprise in his eyes and a knee-weakening smile on his lips, forgetting to paste on the Resting Grump Face in my presence. My heart does a summersault in my chest.

"Yes, I do actually need you to do that. Penny keeps a file of my preferences somewhere," he says, guiding me back to my desk where we rifle through the desk drawer, looking for the alleged Brent Preferences folder. "I think it's a blue folder," he adds.

Penny was supposed to be here to walk me through the transition; instead my boss has to help me perform simple tasks? I grit my teeth. "Whatever happened to Penny training me?" I ask, frustration seeping through my scowl.

He pauses the search, looking almost contrite. "An apartment unexpectedly opened up in Bakersfield, so I told her to go make a quick trip to look at it." He clears his throat. "According to Penny, the apartment market is cutthroat up there and she couldn't let this amazing deal slip through her fingers."

Seeing this caring side of Brent—the one that gives his assistant an unexpected day off—reminds me of the pre-Debacle Brent. The sweet boy next door I fell for in high school. Looking back at my fifteen-year-old self, I wonder if that Libby jumped to conclusions too quickly.

Our hands graze as we both reach for a blue folder hiding at the bottom of the drawer. An electrical charge zaps between us, even though we're standing on a hardwood floor. Brent hands me the folder as if nothing happened.

"Why isn't this stored on your shared drive?" I huff, reacting to the fact that he seems oblivious to the attraction I feel towards him.

"Penny wasn't as tech savvy as you. Although storing the file on our shared drive is an excellent suggestion," he says.

I scan the folder, arching an eyebrow and suppressing a smirk. "Everything is written on yellow stickies?"

He tugs at the collar of his shirt. "Um, well, that was my system with Penny. Every time I thought of a new preference, I left her a sticky on her desk."

I smack him in the chest with the folder like I would have done when we were kids, then my eyes go wide realizing I just hit the boss. "Sorry Mr. Masterson, I didn't mean to clobber you with the folder."

A belly laugh rumbles out of his mouth and he playfully grabs the folder from me. We tussle over the folder for several seconds, back and forth, back and forth, laughing like teenagers until a gray-haired lady strolls by, giving us a disapproving side-eye glare.

I abruptly let go of the folder and take a couple steps back, then cringe, knowing that the office is going to be buzzing about Brent and his new assistant. We need to keep things professional between us while we're at the office, especially if I have any hope of not falling for him.

Brent clears his throat, "We should probably keep things professional between us while we're at the office."

Duh. My thoughts exactly.

I salute and he turns on his heel to disappear back into his lair.

"Honestly that's the dumbest system I've ever heard of, sir," I add. He glances back to see me holding up the blue folder with a smug look on my lips. I watch as he suppresses a smile then disappears.

~*~

The next day before Brent leaves on his trip, he flies into the office, two coffees in his hand, and his laptop balanced on his shoulder.

"For you," he says, plopping one cup on my desk, then striding off towards his office.

"Wait! What's this for?"

He pauses, then rotates to face me. "I appreciate you taking the initiative to make my travel arrangements. And you've been a real trouper since Penny bailed and you didn't get any training."

Wow. How did I forget about this side of Brent? Have we been too caught up in our feud to remember why we liked each other all those years ago?

"You're just happy that I scheduled a flight to New York and not New Orleans," I tease.

He laughs. "True. That would have been a problem."

"Do you remember that time you told Griff Becky Roberts had a crush on him and wanted him to take her to the Spring Fling dance, when it was really Becky Robertson with the crush?"

Letting his laptop bag slide to the floor, he leans against the wall and takes a sip from his cup. "In my defense, those two were easy to mix up. Both blondes. Both tall. Both flirty."

I roll my eyes. "One wore glasses and the other one did not. One had braces and the other one did not."

His brow creases. "Really? How did I miss that?"

"Too busy looking at their other attributes?" I suggest.

His neck turns red, and he stares at his cup, refusing to make eye contact. "Which one had glasses and braces?"

Snickering, I say, "Becky Roberts."

"Man, I really messed that up, didn't I?" he mumbles.

I bark out a laugh. "Well don't feel too bad. Becky Robertson got caught smoking behind the school and was expelled for a week. Ended up Becky Roberts was the only choice to take to the dance."

Brent straightens. "If I remember right, Griff and Becky with Braces had a good time anyway." His chest puffs out with pride.

I nod. "Although his first choice would have been Arielle."

"Ah, yes, his lovely fiancée. How are Griff and Ari doing?" A cloudy expression crosses his face. Unfortunately, since Griff's injury, Brent's relationship with my brother has been strained. I don't even know that they've talked since Griff retired.

"Griff created an app for Ari's company, and it's selling like gangbusters."

Another expression flits over his face, he picks up his laptop, and turns back towards his office. "I'm glad he's happy and using that computer science degree of his."

I feel a sudden pang of regret. First my relationship with Brent never recovered from The Debacle and now Griff and Brent's friendship hasn't recovered after Griff's injury. Maybe all of us need to admit our mistakes and move on. Is that possible?

In just the first week of working for him, Brent's wormed his way back into my heart. Maybe Maggie is right. There's a fine line between love and hate. Have I been in love with him this whole time?

Nine – The Dating Disaster

Brent

With me going out of town the rest of the week, there's no time to convince Libby to go to the gala with me. Rushing her into the fake dating plan would blow up in my face faster than a lit stick of dynamite. She'd probably resign as well, leaving me with a worse headache.

I scrounge up Aspen's phone number and make the call to invite her to attend with me. If I remember correctly, she was a respectable date, other than the skimpy dress.

"Hello?" she answers on the first ring.

"Hi Am—er—Aspen. It's Brent Masterson," I say, cringing as I flub her name.

Silence hangs on the line for a couple beats. *Has she forgotten me?*

"Well, well, I never expected you to call again."

A nervous laugh slips out. "I've been rather busy, what with Dad giving me more and more team responsibility."

"Oh?" her voice perks up. "So, you're the team owner now?"

Maybe that's the hook to get her to agree to date me. And I am practically the team owner. Just a few small hurdles to get over. Clearing my throat, I say, "Yes, but it hasn't been announced yet. We must keep it hush hush."

She mutters something on the other end of the line. *Did that sound like "my lips are sealed"?*

Feeling like a big liar, liar, pants on fire—which I am—I add, "I'd love for you to accompany me to the sportswriters gala this next Saturday. I do need to mention that it's a very highbrow crowd, so they're requesting long dresses with no exposed skin, and absolutely no, um, er, well, visible *cleavage*." I wince as that comes out sounding idiotic. I even practiced the spiel several times and then I bungle it like a gawky teen. My voice even cracks on the word *cleavage*.

"Sportswriters are highbrow? Since when?" she fires back.

She focuses on that and not my botched attempt at getting her to wear full coverage attire? Scrambling for a response, I glance at the email on my screen, inviting me and my date to the event. "The invitation is very staid looking and clearly spells out the dress code," I say as I look at the tacky invite sporting a cocktail glass and a silhouette of a very busty woman. My pants are now sporting a four-alarm fire.

"Okay, I suppose I can find *something* appropriate to wear," she says with a put-out sigh. "What time are you picking me up?"

We agree on six o'clock and I hang up. A feeling in the pit of my stomach says that even if I had to drag Libby to the event kicking and screaming it would go better than a date with Amber, er, Aspen.

~*~

The night starts off on a good note when Aspen meets me at the door wearing a long flowy dress with long sleeves and a high neckline. There's more material in the sleeve of this dress than her previous outfit. It outlines her every curve, but at least there's no exposed skin or *cleavage*.

"You look very nice," I say.

She quirks both eyebrows. "Thanks for the gushing compliment."

Deciding I'd just stick my foot in my mouth if I said more, I usher her into the waiting limo. My driver, Charlie, nods affably. He's driven me to many of these affairs, always the consummate professional, never commenting on any of my dates.

"Got any drinks?" Aspen asks the minute her butt hits the leather seat.

I slide over to the little fridge on the other side of the car. "There's beer, water, and soda."

She wrinkles her nose. "I guess a beer will do."

Twisting off the cap, I hand her the beer. She guzzles her drink while ignoring me and scrolling on her phone. The image reminds me of why I didn't ask her out again, because she acted like this on our first date. She doesn't care a fig about me, this is simply an opportunity to see and be seen. Maybe she'll shape up once we're inside the fancy hotel.

Ten minutes later I get the answer to that question. Aspen becomes Miss Congeniality as we stroll through the crowded room. When people I know stop me for a quick chat, Aspen clings to my arm and hangs on to their every word. She ignores the women and bats her eyes at the men, giggling loudly at their distasteful jokes.

"This is really a see and be seen event, isn't it? And to think I'm here with the team owner!"

Thankfully there's a lot of noise in the room and no one overhears her comment. I fight down the urge to reach over and clamp a hand over her mouth. "Remember, we have to keep that on the down low until it's officially announced," I remind her.

She makes a motion with her fingers, locking her lips, and gives me a playful wink. As her eyes scan around the room, her brows draw together. "I thought you said there was a dress code?" Scantily clad women cling to tuxedo clad men, giving no credence to me insisting she wear conservative attire.

Pointing to myself I say, "I'm wearing a tuxedo." Aspen gives me a stink-eye look that could melt the intricate ice sculpture featured at the beverage bar.

Out of the corner of my eye, I see Mom and Dad approach, creating a timely diversion. Hopefully they don't recognize Aspen since she's covered from neck to toe.

"Son, who's your date?" Dad asks, eyeing her closely.

"I want you to meet Aspen . . . Aspen, my mom and dad." My mind blanks on her last name, assuming I ever knew it.

"It's so nice to meet you! Brenty has told me everything about you!" Aspen enthuses.

Brenty? Where did that come from?

Mom gives Dad a side-eye glance filled with disapproval. But they both politely shake Aspen's hand. Hopefully we aren't all sitting at the same table; that would spell disaster.

The emcee announces everyone should take their seats for dinner. Five minutes later, we're seated at a table with Mom and Dad, plus several of their close friends. My stomach ties into knots, and I'm not sure I'll be able to eat.

Dinner goes smoothly, probably because Aspen is too busy snarfing down food rather than making conversation. She utters an occasional "yum" or "oh so good" and smacks her lips, but most of the table occupants don't seem to notice. I can't decide whether Mom's stink-eye is directed at my date or me or both.

Unfortunately, Aspen downs three glasses of wine as quickly as she devours the steak and shrimp. After glass three, she's definitely tipsy. She openly flirts with me, continuing to call me Brenty and leaning into my personal space. She's so close I can see every lash of her fake eye lashes.

"Did you know Brenty is the big boss man now?" Aspen asks, addressing everyone at the table. *Hic! Hic!* She puts her hand over her mouth and giggles, but the hiccups keep coming. *Hic! Hic!*

Laughing nervously, I say, "Aspen likes to exaggerate! I may have mentioned that I'm Manager of Player Personnel." I state my current title in hopes that Aspen will catch on.

Her forehead creases. "What? I thought you were—"

"Oh look! Here comes dessert!" I leap from my chair and grab a dessert plate off an unsuspecting server's tray. The guy looks like he's going to protest, but I quickly plop the chocolate cake down in front of Aspen and hand her a fork. "I know how much you love chocolate."

The server moves on while Aspen frowns and the rest of the table looks at me as if I've lost my mind. Eventually the cake distracts my date, and she accepts the fork and tucks into the dessert with gusto. "This is so good!" she says between mouthfuls.

Wishing desperately I had a person on standby to call me with a fake excuse to leave, I rack my brain for how to end this evening as gracefully as possible.

My date provides the perfect out when she spills her next glass of red wine down the front of her dress.

"Oops!" she says, then laughs like a hyena.

All eyes around the table lock on Aspen and me. One of Dad's golf buddies sitting next to Aspen hands her his napkin. Mom's friend Mrs. Feldman suggests using club soda to remove the stain. She even looks around the room like she's going to flag down a server.

"I better get Amber home so she can fix her dress," I exclaim, leaping to my feet.

"Isn't her name Aspen?" Mom says.

Treating the question as a rhetorical one, I help ASPEN to her feet, murmur my apologies to the table for leaving early, and flee like the building is on fire. Once we're safely back in the limo, Aspen leans on me and falls asleep.

Dad's going to chew my butt out from here to Cincinnati.

~*~

As predicted, my presence is requested at Mom and Dad's the next day for Sunday brunch. When I arrive, Dad greets me with a scowl. He steers me into the study with barely a hello. *Uh-oh.*

Pointing to the chair across from his desk, he sits and stares at me with steepled fingers before I'm even halfway across the room. Gritting my teeth, I sit and wait for the chewing out.

Dad sighs and his glare softens. "Brent, please tell me you aren't serious about that woman."

My eyes widen. *Maybe this isn't going to be a chewing out but rather a heart-to-heart.* Time for me to pull out the stops. "After last evening, I fear that Am, er, Aspen is not the one for me." *Why can't I get her name right?* Clearing my throat, I plow on since Dad doesn't call me on the name blunder. "I wish I could see my way clear to ignoring her drinking problem, but I simply can't. Dad, I may need more time to find "the one" as obviously I've had a bit of a setback."

Dad snorts. "Nice try. You aren't taking this ultimatum very seriously, are you?"

Am I that transparent? Suppressing the desire to both grimace and whine, I say, "It's harder than you think. She only dated me because she thought I was now the owner of the team. I saw dollar signs flash in her eyes."

Dad grunts. "Look harder. There's plenty of nice women out there, you just aren't looking in the right place." He steeples his fingers under his chin, giving me a steely stare. "There's a charity auction next weekend. Mom and I expect you to bring a suitable date, and you better know her name."

My neck heats. There's no fooling my parents, they're like a pair of trained bloodhounds, hot on the trail of Brent's quest for finding *the one.* I better not only bring someone suitable, but someone I could actually fall for.

Libby's face pops into my mind again. I need to step up my game and convince her into the fake dating scheme. She'd never embarrass me like Aspen did. A queasiness settles in my stomach knowing I could fall for Libby quite easily. Can I fake date her without any emotional consequences?

Dad stands, indicating the discussion is over. "Now, let's go eat Mom's quiche and talk about how we're going to get Sam Hudson to sign his contract extension."

My palms sweat knowing I've got only a few days to persuade Libby that fake dating is a wonderful idea. Maybe I'll just yank off the Band Aid, explain the bind I'm in, and ask her to help me out. *That should be easy, right?*

Ten – The Fake Dating Scheme

Libby

Brent strolls into the office on Monday and says, "Um, so, I have a little favor to ask." His face heats as he shifts back and forth on his feet. I recognize this as his tell for being nervous; he did this when he asked me to prom. The smooth and suave Brent Masterson is still nervous around *me?*

My brows knit. "What kind of favor?" I spurt out through pursed lips, expecting the worst. Am I going to be running off on some personal errand? Why didn't I make it clear from the onset that I'm not his errand girl?

He winces at my blunt reply. "Please come into my office for a minute and I'll explain."

Possibilities swirl in my mind as I follow him into his office. I sit while he flops unceremoniously into the oversized office chair behind his desk, as if his legs can no longer support him. This favor must be a doozie.

We stare at each other across the broad mahogany surface. A tiny smidgen of compassion hits me at how distressed Brent appears to be over this favor. He tugs at his collar, adjusts the cuffs on his shirt—one by one, then taps a pen on his desk. His delay tactics are starting to make me nervous.

Tap. Tap. Tap.

"Get on with it!" I yell, trying to yank him out of this nervous stupor.

The pen tumbles from his fingers and his eyes widen. "Um, right," he says, then clears his throat and straightens his cuffs again. With his eyes firmly focused on his desk, Brent says, "Well, you're probably going to laugh, but I was wondering if you'd go to a charity auction with me next weekend."

My eyes grow big as saucers. This was the last thing I was expecting the favor to be. Thoughts of cleaning his apartment, running out to buy more toner, or picking up his dry cleaning all came to mind. But not this.

"Can't one of your usual bimbos go?" I fire back, then bite my lip at my lack of tact.

Brent cringes. "Dad commented unfavorably on my usual date choices, so I thought I'd switch it up. Take someone he won't expect."

That's a load of hogwash if I've ever heard it. Crossing my arms over my chest, I say, "Come clean, Masterson. That's not the real reason and you know it."

A loud sigh escapes, as Brent slumps back in his chair. He stares at me for several ticks as the gears turn in his head. "I've got to find a genuine girlfriend—someone who could be the future Mrs. Masterson—and get engaged in six months or else Dad's going to sell the team."

If my eyes could pop out of my head, they would. "And you think I'm a good choice? How on earth is this even feasible?"

He holds up a placating hand. "We'd only be fake dating. We can still hate each other in private, but in public we would look like a happy loving couple."

My nose crinkles. Why am I even considering this? I stare at his handsome despairing face, my heart flips, and any resistance I planned on surmounting crumbles. The fine line between love and hate has just become finer, and I suspect I'm already on the side that's going to jeopardize my heart.

"Do we have to hold hands?" I ask, planting a frown on my face.

"Yes."

"How about kissing?" My frown deepens.

The leather in his chair squeaks loudly when he shifts his weight. "Maybe?"

I scramble to think of a sufficiently dour response before my mind can take off into a daydream about the feel of his lips on mine and his arms around my waist. "Is this the real reason you hired me?" I ask in a dejected voice. *Now that I think about it, that does actually hurt.* The daydream vanishes in a puff of smoke.

Our eyes lock and this time he doesn't squirm under my intense glare. "Yes, partly," he admits quietly.

Surging to my feet, I point a finger at him. "That's crummy, Brent and you know it!" My lips wobble as I turn to run from his office and from the building.

"Libby, wait! Do you really want to go back to Harv's Diner?"

My steps halt. A vision of that hideous uniform floats through my mind. Brent's playing his trump card and he knows it.

"Come on. Please sit back down and let's discuss this like mature adults," Brent says in a tone that's a blend between begging and contrition.

Hardening my heart, I march back to the chair and perch on the edge of the seat, my lips set in a mutinous frown. Fake dating Brent is only marginally better than working at Harv's Diner, but fake dating aside, I do actually like this job. "I'll do it on two conditions."

A small grin lights his face, and he nods. "What conditions?"

"No real kissing. A peck on the cheek, but nothing more." *All of my resolve will 100 percent melt if his lips meet mine.*

The look on his face is unreadable. "Okay."

My heart dips at his quick acquiescence. A small part of me wanted him to push back on that one. At least negotiate for an occasional touch of lips. *Guess he's not attracted to me. This really is mercenary.* I press on. "And I want a raise. You can call it hazard pay."

"You just started two weeks ago!" he shoots back.

I dig in my heels. "Take it or leave it, Masterson."

He plays with that darn pen again as he ponders my last condition. *Tap. Tap. Tap.* For a brief moment I almost withdraw my request. I really need this job. But my ego still stings that he only hired me as a way to convince his dad that he found a girlfriend, one that he has a future with. I'm merely a pawn in his scheme to take ownership of the team.

The tapping stops and his eyes narrow when he's made a decision. "I agree to your conditions. You define the amount of your hazard pay and I'll add that to your contract. But you only get it if we convince Dad our fake engagement is real."

I sigh. "After we convince him and he fully hands over the team to you, what's the plan with us?" I point between Brent and me.

"We stage a fight and break up. Come to think of it, that's probably the easiest part of the plan," he says with a smirk. "It's fake dating, Libby. Real emotions won't be involved."

A vision of throwing a diamond engagement ring at his insufferable head surprisingly makes my spirits droop. Is it going to be as easy as he thinks to keep our emotions out of this fake dating scheme? *Do it for the job, Libby.*

"You have a deal, Mr. Masterson." I stand and extend my hand.

He stands and we shake. A tingle runs up my arm and neck, but I ignore it. *I'm no longer attracted to Brent Masterson! Certainly not after the shenanigans he just pulled.*

Eleven – Fake Dating Rules

Brent

Now that Libby knows about the fake dating scheme and has reluctantly agreed to it—at a steep price, I must say—there's even more awkwardness between us. We're like two actors in a play where we don't know the script. We bungle our way through the rest of the day.

"Brent, or should I call you Mr. Masterson or sir while we're at the office?" Libby says, hesitating at my door.

"Does it matter?" I ask, arching an eyebrow.

She waves her hand. "Never mind. Since it appears that Penny is never going to train me, while you were on your trip, I looked through the computer and her desk, and I think I've figured everything out."

I pinch the bridge of my nose. "I'm sorry Libby, with that trip, I forgot all about the training. Penny called me and begged for more time off. Turns out they didn't get that apartment and she needed more time to hunt."

"I didn't know Bakersfield was such a real estate hotbed," Libby says with a snort. "I wouldn't want to stand between Penny and her perfect apartment."

I can't tell if she's joking or mad at me. We stare at each other for a few ticks, then she laughs, breaking the tension.

"Would it be okay if I just pay Penny her last week and tell her not to bother to come in?" I ask.

Libby shrugs. "Sure. Like I said, I've got this, boss, er, Mr. Masterson." She turns to leave.

"Was that all you wanted?"

She bites her lip, pausing for a few beats. "Will your dad really sell the team if you don't find a real girlfriend in six months?"

Leaning back in my chair, I sigh. "Who knows. He's threatening that."

"What would you do if you didn't have the team to manage?" Libby asks, with what looks like genuine concern on her face.

She's somehow hit on the thing that scares me the most. *What would I do if I didn't manage the team?* I went straight from college to working for Dad. My marketing degree would need a lot of dusting off if I hoped to use it. I shrug, but I don't think I hide my feelings very well.

Her eyes bore into mine for a few more seconds, then she nods as if coming to an internal decision. "I'll do everything I can to make this fake dating thing work, Brent. I owe you that much for saving me from Harv's Diner."

Guilt slams into me. My reasons for hiring her were not altruistic, yet she's thanking me. "We can have fun. You'll like the auction and all the quirky stuff to bid on."

She grins. "Whatever I bid on will be with your dime, Mr. Masterson." Flipping her hair over her shoulder, she disappears back to her desk, and I grin. Now I'm looking forward to the auction.

~*~

On day two after Libby agreed to the fake dating scheme, she strolls into my office, lets out a big sigh, and plops into the guest chair. "I think we need some more guidelines and rules about this fake dating thing," she says. "I worried about it all night."

"Do I need to write a handbook?" I tease.

She purses her lips and tosses me a frowny librarian scowl. "No! Of course not. But I have some scenarios I'd like to talk through." Flipping open the notebook in her hand, she starts to read from a page filled with notes. "Number One, I prefer that we show no signs of attraction around the office or when I'm acting in the capacity of your assistant. No terms of endearment. No flirting. Absolutely no hand holding."

I sink back in my chair, steepling my fingers under my chin. "What if we're at the office but around people who know we're dating, such as Dad? Won't he think it odd that we don't show any affection towards each other? We need this to be believable."

Libby's scowl deepens. "Can't we keep it simple? At work, you're the boss and I'm the employee, and we treat each other as such. No exceptions. You can explain that to your dad as a smart HR practice."

She has me there.

This boss and employee fake dating scheme is getting more complicated by the minute. I should have thought this through better.

"So, at work do you want to call me Mr. Masterson or Brent?" I ask, trying to get more clarification on the line between us.

"Great suggestion! Let's keep it at Mr. Masterson."

That wasn't necessarily what I was going for, but ok. "What do I call you? Miss Griffin? Ms. Griffin? Libby?"

She groans. "I'd prefer you call me Libby."

"Ah ha! I'd be breaking your own rule," I say in a snarky voice.

Chewing on the end of her pen, she ponders my comment for several beats. "Okay, Miss Griffin it is," she says as she scribbles in the notebook. "Number Two, what constitutes fake dating? Do we go out to dinner or to movies together? Things like that? Or does the fake dating scheme only come into play for public events like the charity auction we're attending next weekend?"

I pinch the bridge of my nose. She's making my head hurt. "What do you prefer?"

Looking down at her notebook, she says, "How about we confine the fake dating to public events only?"

I shrug. "Sure. But what about if the two of us grab a quick lunch together during the workday? Or I ask you to meet me for dinner so we can talk shop. Is that fake dating or just working together?"

Her shoulder's slump. "This is the worst idea you've ever had, Brent, er, Mr. Masterson. Let's abide by rules One and Two and then add any addendums, as we go along." She jumps to her feet and exits my office, abruptly ending the conversation. A few seconds later, I hear her typing furiously on her keyboard. No more than a minute later my computer dings with an incoming email from Libby with a Subject line: Fake Dating Rules, Version 1.

I laugh and shake my head.

~*~

The first test of our new rules happens the very next morning.

Libby's sitting at her desk positioned right outside my office when I hear Mom's voice. I immediately go on high alert, wondering why Mom is here. She hardly ever visits, so this is a big surprise to say the least.

"Hello Libby, dear! I was so happy to hear that you'll be accompanying Brent to the charity auction next weekend. It's wonderful to see that you two have patched up your differences. You are perfect for each other!" Mom's voice carries loudly up and down the hall, her enthusiasm evident in every syllable.

Oops!

I may have mentioned to Mom that I was bringing Libby to the auction event after my nosy mother called me last evening and interrogated me about my date. After the Aspen disaster, Mom was doing her due diligence. But I started to sweat over the drilling and dropped Libby's name out of self-preservation.

Springing to my feet, I rush out of my office. Several heads peek out of their offices up and down the hall, watching the events unfolding by my assistant's desk. Uh-oh, tongues are going to be wagging after this.

Libby's sporting an embarrassed blush and looking like she wants to crawl in a hole. "Nice to see you again, Mrs. Masterson," she says. Her eyes dart over to mine, silently questioning the fact Mom knows about the date while at the same time pleading for help.

Sliding over right beside Libby's desk, I turn adoring eyes towards her. "Sweetie, I'm sorry, I spilled the beans to Mom last night." The words float out of my mouth before I can stop them.

Libby's glare would peel paint, but she quickly transforms it into a bright smile. "Snookums, I knew you wouldn't be able to keep us a secret for very long!"

She bats her eyelashes at me and I almost choke. A coughing fit hits as I try to recover from my surprise.

"Shall I get you a bottled water, sir? Er, dearie?"

Mom stares between us, a look of confusion on her face. Libby and I are really messing this up.

I plaster a smile on my face. "I told Libby to address me formally when we're at work. It gets kind of confusing," I croak.

Libby and I turn beaming smiles towards Mom, then Libby gives me a swift kick from behind the desk, out of Mom's vision. My beaming smile slips slightly when her shoe contacts my shin. *Ouch!*

"Mom, your visit is unexpected! Please come into my office so we can chat." I gently take Mom's arm and usher her towards my door.

Mom waves at Libby, then we walk together towards my office, me trying to hide my limp.

"I'm so excited that you are dating such a nice girl like Libby! Your father and I can't wait to see where that leads." Mom's voice drifts back to my new assistant and she hears every word, which was probably Mom's intent.

I shoot Libby an apologetic look over my shoulder. The searing look Libby gives me would singe wood. *Oops. I'm in trouble now.*

Mom chats about inconsequential things such as a new potato salad recipe she's going to try—one she got from Aunt Shirley, making me instantly decide to steer clear of that side dish—and whether our new neighbors are mafia criminals what with all the fancy cars coming and going. I can't even get a word in edgewise, leading me to conclude that Mom's visit was to ferret out my charity auction date, double-check that I didn't just make it up that I'm bringing Libby.

"Oh my! I need to hustle on to my lunch with Laverne and Shirley!" Mom says after about ten minutes of wasting my time. I want to warn her about the pair's new penchant for substitutions but bite my lip.

After Mom leaves, Libby rushes into my office, sputtering like a wet hen. "Brent— Mr. Masterson— sir! Why didn't you warn me that you told your mom about us?" She points furiously between us. "The fake us!"

I hold up a restraining hand. "Mom hardly ever visits. It didn't even occur to me to warn you."

Her eyes shoot daggers.

We glare at each other for several awkward beats. "I'm sorry," I say meekly, staring at Libby's beautiful but angry face. "I'll email you all the details about the charity event," I add as if that makes up for my slip-up with Mom.

The steam goes out of her expression, her scowl morphs into a more detached professional look. "That will be helpful," she mutters. "Don't let this happen again," she says. "We just violated rule Number One. Big time."

"I'll try to do better, sweetie," I say, keeping a straight face.

She rolls her eyes. "May I remind you, sir, of rule Number One? No flirting and no terms of endearment in the office?"

"Ah, right. I'll try to do better, Miss Griffin."

"Thank you, Snookums," she adds with a playful smirk as she retreats to her desk. My eyes are glued to her every movement, and I have to force myself to look away before she sees me staring. Libby is slowly worming her way into my heart, and my resistance to her weakens with every interaction. This fake dating scheme is going to make it even worse.

Twelve – Crullers

Libby

After Mrs. Masterson's visit, everyone in the office treats me differently, as gossip about Brent's and my relationship spreads like wildfire. Hushed conversations cease when I stroll into the breakroom. A few young female colleagues glare at me as if I'd swiped their boyfriend, although I suspect Brent never dated any of them. One of the male young guns on the player recruitment team gave me a flirty wink, as if I'd date him and Brent at the same time. *Awkward!*

I hide out at my desk for the rest of the day, avoiding Brent and the other employees. Keeping my nose stuck in my computer avoids any further awkwardness. Since he avoids me, I get the sense that he's also grappling with how to handle our professional and fake personal relationships. *Maybe we need more rules?*

Keeping focused on work, I resolve what to do with Penny's crazy colorized scheme for tracking stuff. It's quite humorous, but I won't be adopting it. There are literally colored folders for everything. Like that famous blue Brent Preferences folder. I stack the collection of Crayola-inspired folders on my desk—there's even a manilla folder for tracking expenses. Guess she couldn't come up with a color for those.

Focusing on translating the colored folder scheme into a tracking spreadsheet, I'm determined to bring Brent's office into the digital age.

~*~

I have no time to stew about office gossip the next day either, as Brent's schedule is jam-packed; he's meeting with Sam Hudson and his agent mid-morning, hopefully to sign the star pitcher to a contract extension. Brent hasn't told me anything he needs me to do for the meeting, but I'll ask him when he comes in.

I settle at my desk, and not more than five minutes later Brent rolls in looking like a sick dog. I've never seen him like this—other than in middle school when the entire student population came down with the flu. Griff and Brent were sick for days while I only got a mild case. I pride myself in my ironclad autoimmune system.

He ignores me and heads straight into his office. I jump up and follow him, needing to sort out the upcoming meeting.

"You look terrible, Brent, er, Mr. Masterson." I say as he slumps behind his desk.

He grimaces and grabs his head with both hands. "Please speak quietly," he says through clinched teeth.

"Do you have a hangover?" I whisper.

"No," he groans. "It's the start of a migraine."

Coming to his side, I say, "How bad is it?"

"Horrible," he mumbles into his hands still holding his head.

"I'll be right back." I sprint to my desk and grab the headache medicine from my purse. It's the over-the-counter stuff but that's all I have. When I return, poor Brent is still holding his head. He hasn't moved a muscle.

Grabbing a bottled water from the fridge under his desk, I say, "Here, take two of these."

He meekly holds out his hand, swallows the pills, and gulps down some water. He's pale, and his eyes are red like he hasn't slept a wink.

"Let's get you over to the couch where you can sleep," I say, tugging on his arm, urging him to stand.

He shakes his head. "I've got to type up the Hudson contract," he croaks.

I squint at him. How's he going to type up a contract when he can barely sit up straight? "Is it one of those pre-canned fill-in-the-blank things?" For a brief time before landing the Harv's Diner job, I worked in a real estate office, and that's how their contracts worked.

He nods, wincing in pain at the motion.

"I'll do it," I say, nudging him to his feet. "Where's the information?"

Sliding out his middle desk drawer—the ones you keep pencils and stuff like that in—he points to a yellow sticky. "Everything is written on that."

I suppress a laugh; the man loves his yellow stickies. Tugging his arm again, I steer him to the couch in the far corner of the office. I have to admit this piece of furniture is very comfy, because I used it a few times last week while he was on his trip. Not to sleep, of course, but it makes a nice place to type up meeting notes. Those were also on stickies, so I took it upon myself to put them in Microsoft Word and store them on the shared drive.

He lets me guide him to the couch, surprisingly without complaint or protest. He must be feeling really awful. I help him shrug out of his suit jacket and carefully hang it over the back of a chair. He doesn't want to look like a wrinkled mess for the meeting with Sam and his agent.

Brent refuses to make eye contact while I loosen his tie and pull it from around his neck. This is, what, the fourth time I've touched him in the last ten minutes, in direct contradiction to rule Number One. I convince myself that violating the rules in this case is acceptable. This is an emergency and Brent needs my help.

He plunks down on the sofa, then stretches out. I hope he's comfortable without any blankets. When I place the bottled water on the end table by the sofa so it's within his reach, he's already snoring like a baby.

Clicking Brent's door firmly closed, I scramble back to my desk, swipe my cell and dial.

"Hey sis, what's happening?" Griff says on the first ring.

"I need your help. Brent's meeting with Sam Hudson and his agent this morning and I thought some pastries might be a nice touch." Griff and I already had a lengthy discussion about the wisdom of me working for Brent, so at least we don't have to rehash that again.

Griff chuckles. "To sweeten Sammy up?"

I laugh. Sam is known to be a bit of a sourpuss. "Do you by chance know his favorite pastry?"

After a few seconds' pause, Griff says, "I think I know the perfect thing. Crullers! One time when we were on a road trip to Philly, Sam and I found a little hole-in-the-wall bakery and they had the best crullers." My brother sighs then adds "yum" a couple times. "We went back every morning."

My brows knit, trying to remember the last time I had one of those twisty deep-fried doughnuts. Some nearby bakery must have them. "Anything else? Does he like coffee?"

"Yep, he's a coffee drinker. Strong and black."

"Thanks Griff! You've been a big help. Say hi to Ari for me!" I hang up before he can brag about his sweet fiancée. No time for chitchat.

Flipping through the contacts in my cell, I locate the person I need help from next. Penny left a detailed list of important numbers connected with that person's role in the company, all neatly written on a piece of lined notebook paper and tucked inside a yellow folder.

"Hello? How may I help you?" a deep voice answers.

At least the guy listed as "company driver" is a friendly sort. I've got my fingers crossed that he can help me. "Charlie Fullerton? This is Libby Griffin, Mr. Masterson's new assistant."

He chuckles. "Miss Griffin, please call me Charlie. What do I owe the honor?"

"I need to pick up some crullers and be back in the office in say, thirty minutes—forty minutes, tops. Can you help me?" Glancing at the time on my cell, I start to sweat. I still need to type up that contract and get the conference room set up. This is going to be cutting it close.

"Yes, I know a place. I'll be downstairs with the car in ten minutes."

"Thank you!"

While I wait for Charlie to arrive, I find the canned contract online and fill in the blanks from the yellow sticky. When my cell buzzes with Charlie's arrival, I press Save. All I need to do is review that and print it when I return.

Sprinting to the elevator and regretting my choice of wearing high heels, I nervously press the button. Hopefully the sleeping bear doesn't wake before I get back and wonder where I'm at.

~*~

Charlie is a gem. I see why Brent and his father have employed him as their driver for over twenty-five years.

"Miss Libby, the bakery I've got in mind is only a few blocks away. We should be able to get there and back in your allotted time," the gray-haired gentleman says as he opens the limo door for me.

"I appreciate your help. I'm not as familiar with this area of town," I say after settling into the luxurious backseat.

We chat about Charlie's grandchildren as the limo glides through town. He's expecting grandbaby number five to arrive any day, and he seems as excited about this one as he must have been for the first grandchild.

My heart drops as we pull up outside a hole-in-the-wall establishment. A pot filled with fake Poinsettias sits beside the door despite the fact that Christmas has come and gone, a cellular shade sags at an odd angle in the front window, and the worn sign on the door is, thankfully, flipped to the Open side.

"Don't let the exterior put you off," Charlie says with a chuckle after seeing the expression on my face. "I guarantee you'll find the best crullers in all of California inside."

I nod, then jump out and run into the bakery. My nose does a happy dance and my stomach rumbles the minute I enter. Tantalizing aromas of sugar, cinnamon, and vanilla make me want to buy more than just a dozen crullers. Several other sugar and caffeine seekers are in line, but it's moving at a fast clip.

I barely have time to survey the nearby bakery cases filled with pastries of all shapes and sizes before a server greets me.

"What can I get you?" she says, her friendly tone encouraging me to order a few items for myself.

"I need a dozen crullers," I say, then succumb to the delicious smells and buy myself an apple fritter and a Long John. Yum! My favorites.

Clutching two white pastry bags in my hand, I slide back into the limo. The minute the car pulls away from the curb, I yank the Long John out of the smaller bag and stuff it in my mouth.

"Get everything you needed?" Charlie asks between chuckles.

"Mhm," I say, my mouth too full to respond. This is the freshest, tastiest Long John I've ever had; I savor every bite. Licking my fingers a few beats later, I add, "Thanks for taking me there! That place is a hidden gem."

He nods.

"Do you happen to like apple fritters?" I ask.

Charlie laughs. "I don't know very many people who don't."

"Here, this one is for you," I say, handing the small bag over the divider between riders and driver.

He tries to wave off my offering. "You don't have to do that, Miss Libby."

I laugh. "Charlie, my hips are going to thank you, believe me."

His broad grin reflects in the rearview mirror as he accepts the white bag.

Once we're back at the office, I slide back out of the car, wave to Charlie, then ascend the elevator back to Brent's office. I sag in relief when his office door is still closed. Our visitors are due to arrive in about thirty minutes. That barely leaves me enough time to get the executive conference room set up, make coffee, and review and print the contract. Wouldn't want an extra zero in the offer amount; Brent would kill me.

I take a few calming breaths and get to work.

~*~

At five minutes to the hour, Sam and his agent, a tall beady-eyed man named Adam, stroll into the office. I plaster a welcoming smile on my face. After preparing everything for the meeting, I peeked in and Brent was still sleeping like a baby, so this part of the plan I'll execute myself.

"Hello, gentlemen! Brent's previous meeting is running over a bit, so let's go into the executive conference room," I say, with a sweep of my hand towards the room. As we walk down the hall, I add, "You know how it is when you're negotiating with the next big star. Brent's been on the phone all morning!"

Both men exchange looks.

Good, that's a little incentive for Sam to sign the contract without further delay.

"Please make yourselves comfortable. There's some pastries and coffee to snack on until Brent arrives."

Sam makes a beeline to the table. "You've got crullers? These are my favorite."

"Well, isn't that lucky?" I smile and motion towards the coffee station at the back of the room. When I first started here a few weeks ago, the coffee pot was an ancient ugly gold-colored (who knew it came in that awful color?) Mr. Coffee machine. I replaced it with a fancy new single brew machine. Brent complained about the cost, but I ignored him.

"Please serve yourselves. I'll go pull Brent out of his meeting and we'll be right back."

The men nod and each take a cruller as the coffee machine belches into action, brewing the first cup. The smiles on their faces tell me that they aren't going to mind that Brent's a few minutes late.

Running back down the hall, I open Brent's door and sneak inside.

Now to waken the sleeping bear.

Thirteen – Signing the Star Pitcher

Brent

"Brent, wake up," a familiar voice says while a gentle hand shakes my shoulder.

I slit one eye open to see Libby squatting down in front of my sofa.

What am I doing on the couch?

Popping up into a sitting position, I glance around the room, trying to get my bearings. Reality slams into me and my eyes fly to the clock on the wall.

"Is Sam and his agent here? Why didn't you wake me sooner!" I bellow, struggling to my feet. At least my head doesn't hurt anymore, but I'm late to the meeting to sign our star pitcher to a contract extension. *I can't blow this opportunity!*

"Settle down," Libby says in a soothing voice. "They're in the executive conference room eating pastries and sipping coffee. They know you're running a little late from your previous appointment."

My eyes widen. "What previous appointment?"

Libby waves her hand. "Oh, just a conversation to sign more talent. I told them it ran over a tad bit."

Ignoring her little fib, I stretch my arms over my head, working out the knots in my back, then realize that I feel so much better. A vague memory of Libby giving me some headache medication surfaces. "Did I sleep all this time?"

She pats my shoulder. "You did. Now let's get you ready for the meeting," she says in a crisp voice. She grabs my suit jacket and tie from a nearby chair, helping me into the jacket and handing me the tie.

"You tie this while I grab the printed contract. Take a couple of swigs of the water; that'll help clear your head." She nods to a bottled water on the end table, then disappears.

Relieved that my headache is gone, I get myself put back together. Luckily the suit jacket isn't wrinkled, and it hides all the sleep-created creases in my shirt. I don't even remember taking the jacket off and hanging it up.

When Libby returns, she nods and smiles. "Looks like you're almost ready!" She straightens my tie and runs her fingers through my hair, setting off tingles that run up my neck. "Just a little combing. We don't want them to think you have bed head," she says, smiling up at me.

My heart flips. If I wasn't already late to my meeting, I'd pull her into my arms and kiss her senseless, ignoring rule Number One. Or is that violating rule Number Two?

Never mind.

Before I walk out my door, I say, "Thanks, Libby, er, Miss Griffin."

She smiles. "Go get 'em, Tiger!"

I think that violated rule Number One. Again.

~*~

When I nonchalantly stroll into the executive conference room, Sam and Adam are laughing. An empty plate sits in front of each one.

"Gentlemen, sorry I'm late," I say. Both men stand. "Sam, great to see you," I say as we shake hands. "And Adam, always a pleasure." I shake his clammy hand, wanting to wipe my hand on my pants leg afterwards. He's a slimy agent, and I wish I didn't have to deal with him.

"Your assistant is a real gem. She got my favorite pastry! I haven't had crullers for years," Sam says, sounding like a big kid as he points to the plate in the center of the table. One lone pastry remains—hopefully I can snag it when they leave.

How did Libby know he liked crullers? Lucky guess?

"Would you like another cup before we get started?" Both men nod and go over to the coffee bar to refill their cups. The shiny new coffee machine is a good touch, although I'll never admit that to Libby. Fortunately they accept my offer, as it gives me time to review the contract.

Pulling the paperwork from the folder Libby handed me, I quickly scan it to make sure there are no errors. Don't want there to be an extra zero on the offer line—Dad would kill me. But Libby created it perfectly from that wrinkled sticky I gave her.

That woman deserves a raise! I squash that thought since she's already finagled hazard pay from me.

Sam and Adam join me at the table. "Please sit. I've got the contract right here, and we can get started as soon as you're ready."

"I'm ready to sign right now," Sam says.

My jaw drops, but I quickly snap it shut. *Who knew that some sugar and caffeine is all it would take to push him over the finish line?* Seems a bit too easy, but we have been hashing this deal out over the phone for weeks. I'll take what I can get.

Sliding the contract across the table along with a pen, I smile and say, "Excellent!"

~*~

Once the contract is signed, we chat for a few minutes, then I walk Sam and Adam towards the bank of elevators located just outside my office.

Sam stops at Libby's desk. "Those crullers were delicious, Miss Griffin. May I ask where you got them?"

She gives him a beaming smile and a pang of jealousy hits. "At Edelman's Bakery. It's at the corner of Bayside Drive and Ninety-Fifth."

"Can you text me the address?" Sam asks, as if he can't Google the place himself.

"Of course!" The two of them exchange phone numbers while I watch. Adam has his nose stuck in his phone, paying no attention to any of us.

Sam's overt flirting spurs me to take an objective look at my assistant. Libby looks professional yet very attractive in her blouse and skirt. Those high heels really showcase her legs. If I'm honest, she's beautiful. *No wonder he's hitting on her.*

Sam is one of the biggest flirts I know, and this request for the bakery information is just a ruse to get her phone number. I'll warn Libby about him once they leave.

"We'll email you a copy of the contract," I add as the men enter the elevator, the doors gliding shut.

Strolling back to Libby's desk, I see she's already focused on her computer, typing animatedly. I set the folder with the signed contract on the edge of her desk, and she finally looks up.

"Can you scan this and email a copy to Sam and Adam?"

She nods. "Yes, Mr. Masterson."

I sigh. "Can we amend rule Number One?"

Arching an eyebrow, she says, "What do you suggest?"

"Call me Brent and I'll call you Libby."

A small grin tips her lips. "Certainly, sir, er, Brent."

I chuckle and head towards my office. Turning I say, "By the way, thanks for saving my butt. I was in no condition to meet with those two, and you handled everything. Thank you."

She blushes. "Of course. That's why I'm here."

After I settle at my desk—a goofy smile lighting my face—my computer dings. Opening my Inbox, I see an email from Libby with the subject: Fake Dating Rules, Version 2.

I laugh.

Fourteen – Is it Couture?

Libby

"Why the frowny face, amiga?" Maggie says when she strolls into our apartment after work. Today was a rare occasion when she had to be in the office. She's dressed to the nines in a figure-hugging business suit.

Deflecting her question, I say, "I bet your boss noticed you in that!" Maggie has a crush as long as my arm on her boss, and I can't help but tease her.

She sinks down on the sofa, blowing out a loud breath. "He looks at me as if I'm office furniture! Nothing I do breaks through his professional exterior."

"Does your office have HR rules against dating? Maybe he's just trying not to break the rules. Especially since he's your boss." I frown, thinking about my inept attempt at creating rules for Brent and me to follow when we're in the office. All the rules accomplish is to make things more awkward.

How am I supposed to remember whether to call him sir, Mr. Masterson, or Brent? Obviously, I need to print off Version 2, with updates highlighted in red, and hang it on his wall so we can refer to it.

She chews on her lip. "Well, technically he's not exactly my boss. Our team got reorganized into another group."

My eyes widen. "When did that happen?"

She shrugs. "A few weeks ago. But he still doesn't notice me beyond my role as project manager."

Believe me, most men notice Maggie. Whenever we go out to eat together, men of all ages hit on her. The waiter . . . The guy sitting at the table next to us at the restaurant . . . A random dude walking past us on the street. It's mildly infuriating—I feel like the ugly stepsister beside her.

"Give him time, he's probably still adjusting to the reorganization."

"Maybe. So, what about you? How's the fake relationship with hunky Mr. Masterson progressing?" She waggles her eyebrows and grins.

I told her about the fake dating rules, but I haven't told her yet about the charity auction. "Well, actually I need your help. I'm going to a charity thing with him this weekend and I need your advice on what to wear."

She lets out a loud squeal and does an energetic fist pump. Then she just as quickly turns serious. "That's cutting it close! Let's go shopping after work tomorrow!"

Of course the fashionista wants to shop, but I don't think my wallet will agree with that. "I was hoping to wear something I already own."

Her nose wrinkles as if she smells something bad. "What do you have that's suitable?"

"How about the dress I wore to the Nutcracker Suite performance last Christmas?"

She shakes her head. "Sorry, amiga, but you look like a nun in that thing."

Do I? I stare at my roomie for a few seconds trying to decide if the dress is that bad or if Maggie just wants an excuse to shop. Her expression suggests the dress is that bad.

"Okay, we can go look. But I'm sticking to whatever we can find in my closet if we strike out after one hour."

Maggie beams, rubbing her hands together. "Trust me, we'll find something much better!"

~*~

The after-work crowds aren't as bad as I expected. Thank goodness it isn't Christmas shopping season because I couldn't tolerate that.

Maggie and I have gone to three different stores so far without success, so my spirits are flagging.

"The red dress will have to do," I say in a grumpy voice, slouching down on the little bench inside the women's dressing room.

"Oh no! That won't do! We just haven't found the one yet," Maggie says.

How does she still have all this energy and positivity? I'm hangry. How close are we to my hour limit?

"I've tried on seventeen dresses. That's my limit."

"I feel like number eighteen is the lucky one! Let me make another pass through the dress section." She scurries off before I can protest.

Pulling a granola bar out of my purse, I eat it, contemplating how terrible the red dress would be. When I bought it, I loved the flared skirt and long sleeves that cover me from chin to mid-calf. But I understand Maggie's comment about looking like a nun after scrolling the internet to see what other women have worn to this charity event in the past.

While I'd never wear anything as skimpy as some of them, the dresses all scream couture or designer labels. Sparkly little numbers guaranteed to turn heads. Maggie's right, the red dress simply won't cut it. My heart rate ticks up as I start to panic. What if we can't find The Dress? The memory of prom dress shopping with Grams pushes itself into my head. Sadly, I never got to wear that dress; just another fallout from The Debacle.

"You have to try this one!" Maggie flies into the dressing room with a dress clutched in her hand and hangs it up for me to see. Her smile is as broad as her face, and she rubs her hands in excitement.

The shimmery silver dress does fit the bill in terms of flashiness. The hemline is short, very short. It covers only one shoulder, leaving the other shoulder bare. I've never worn anything as fancy (or revealing) as this before.

"It looks kind of short," I say, finishing my last bite of granola bar.

Maggie smirks. "You've got great legs, Libby. Why would you cover them up?" She stares at me with a challenge in her eyes.

Ugh! Folding under her scrutiny, I carefully remove the dress from the hanger. It feels light and silky to the touch. My friend helps me tug the gorgeous dress over my head—without her assistance I'm sure I would have put my head through the wrong hole.

The minute I turn around to look in the mirror, I'm in love.

"Oh my!" I say in awe. The hemline hits me mid-thigh, but it's not so daringly short that I won't be able to sit down. The dress makes me look like a celebrity, a stylish, well-dressed woman not afraid to show a little skin but not exposing too much. I don't look tacky, and even Gramps wouldn't call out the dress as too skimpy.

It's perfect.

"Yes, oh my goodness! You look so pretty in that. The color goes perfectly with your brunette hair," Maggie gushes.

We stand side by side and both smile into the mirror, knowing this is The Dress.

"Now! Let's go get some killer heels to wear with it!" Maggie springs into action before I can look at the price tag and talk myself out of the beautiful creation. She whips the dress back over my head. Once I'm dressed back in my street clothes, she tugs me over to the shoe department. She's like a tornado and I'm caught in her path, but I don't resist.

My heart beats excitedly. I'm going to feel like Cinderella at the ball . . . *A fake ball.*

Reality slams into me. My carriage is going to turn into a pumpkin and my prince and I are going to break up once his dad fully turns the team over to him. No happily ever after like in the fairy tale.

Thrusting those depressing thoughts aside, I decide to enjoy the ride while I can.

Fifteen – Cinderella at the Ball

Brent

This fake dating, all of Libby's rules, and trying to work together is *awkward*. Tonight though, we can ignore the rules. This is a date, albeit a fake one, and we can interact like a normal couple. Hold hands. Dance. Flirt. Maybe I can even steal a kiss if I play my cards right. Clearly she's amenable to rule changes since we're already up to Version 2. Ever since she saved my bacon with Sam, I'm determined not to pay any attention to Libby's assertion that all I can do is give her a peck on the cheek.

Why did I agree to that dumb condition?

The limo pulls up outside my condo. Charlie, my driver, opens the door so I can climb inside. He's been with the organization for so many years, we've become friendly acquaintances.

"Good evening, sir. Shall we go straight away to pick up your date?"

"Yes. Do you have her address?"

"Yes, Miss Libby provided it."

When did Charlie meet my assistant?

Charlie settles behind the wheel and the long black sleek vehicle pulls away, gliding through town. It's a pleasure to ride in such luxury and not have to deal with traffic myself.

"Do you know Libby?" I ask, not able to contain my curiosity any longer.

"Yes, I met her when she bought the pastries for your meeting with Sam Hudson. She was in quite a tizzy and needed to find crullers in less than thirty minutes! It just so happens those are also my favorite, so I knew exactly where to go."

I didn't realize how much effort Libby went to in order to save my butt that morning. It never occurred to me that she picked up the pastries herself. I thought she had them delivered.

"The pastries were a big hit," I say.

The limo driver chuckles. "Sounds like they did the trick. You got Sam to sign the extension."

True. Without the crullers to sweeten them up, Sam or Adam might have wanted to re-negotiate the terms. Again. Libby dropping that little fib about my phone call to an up-and-coming star probably also helped. I grin.

She's like a secret weapon.

"Sir, may I speak honestly?"

"Sure," I reply, wondering what's coming next.

"Your assistant is a real gem. You shouldn't let her get away."

My eyes widen, since this is the first time my driver has given me any advice, dating or otherwise. "Thanks for the advice, Charlie. I'll take it under advisement."

He laughs. "She's not like those other women you've been taking to these shindigs. I'm going to bet she isn't wearing a dress with less material than a handkerchief. Libby is a real classy lady."

I don't know if he's warning me to be on my best gentlemanlike behavior or what. "I agree. Libby is one special lady."

Charlie nods, my reply seeming to satisfy him as he concentrates on driving. On the other hand, my nerves ratchet up as we approach Libby's apartment. By the time we arrive, my palms are damp, and I may have sweated through my fancy shirt. I wonder why I'm never this nervous when taking one of those skimpily dressed strangers to an event like this.

I jump out of the limo almost before Charlie's parked at the curb. Trying to stem my excitement, I take calming breaths and walk in measured steps to her front door.

One, two, buckle my shoe,
Three, four, knock at the door.

Why this silly nursery rhyme pops into my head, I don't know. But oddly it helps settle my nerves and keeps me from sprinting up the sidewalk.

Five, six, pick up sticks,
Seven, eight, lay them straight,
Nine, ten, a big fat hen—

Thankfully I get to the door before *eleven, twelve* because I can't remember the rest of this ridiculous rhyme. I raise my hand to knock—

"Amigo! Please come inside. Libby is almost ready." A Latina woman about the same age as Libby answers the door. She yanks me inside; her exuberant greeting makes my nerves kick up again. "You must be Brent! I've heard so much about you. I'm Margarite Consuelo DiSilva Coronado, Libby's roommate."

Her handshake nearly pulls my arm from its socket, and my fingers ache afterwards. Fleetingly I wonder whether she played baseball as a kid, considering her outstanding hand strength.

I finally come to my senses and return her greeting. "Nice to meet you," I say, although I've already forgotten her long list of names.

She eyes me like a stern father measuring up his daughter's date. I feel sweat forming on my brow at her scrutiny, but I return her stare, trying to keep a pleasant expression on my face. After a few awkward beats, she says, "You can call me Maggie."

I feel like I just passed a test—relief sets in despite the fact that I don't know what I did to satisfy her. "Maggie," I repeat, then cringe. It sure isn't my scintillating conversation that got me past the roommate test.

This woman is intense. Hope I never get on her bad side.

She smirks. "Let me go check on Cinderella!" she bellows, then runs off down the hall.

I grin at her reference to the fairy tale. Taking my phone from my pocket while I wait, I scan ESPN news for baseball-related stories. Sam Hudson's contract extension made headlines earlier in the week, so I'm checking for any pundit reactions. A noise catches my attention, and I glance up.

Wowza!

Libby's standing there wearing a stunning silver off-the-shoulder dress that takes my breath away. She chews on her bottom lip and gives me a shy smile. The roomie is hovering in the background, grinning from ear to ear.

My brain kicks into action and I find my voice. "Libby, you look stunning," I say, walking towards her and taking her hand. Gazing into her eyes, I'm struck by her understated beauty. She looks sexier than any of those women I've dated in the past, and her dress is modest by comparison.

"Thank you. I'm ready," she says, grabbing a tiny clutch purse from the end table.

We walk hand-in-hand to the limo. I keep glancing over at her, happiness and pride flowing through me that she's my date. I help her slide inside the long vehicle—her short dress and high heels hamper her movements, but she manages to get in without mishap.

"Good evening, Charlie! How are you doing?" Libby asks once the vehicle is in motion.

"Doing well, Miss Libby," my driver replies.

"Has grandbaby number five made an appearance yet?"

Charlie chuckles. "Not yet. He's being stubborn."

He has grandchildren? I feel a pang of guilt that Libby knows more about Charlie's private life than I do. Resolving to learn more about Charlie's personal life another time, I slide closer to her on the soft and comfy leather seats. The limo feels like you're riding down the street on your sofa.

Libby smiles at me, my heart flips, and I become tongue-tied again. For a guy who runs a multimillion-dollar organization, I sure am acting like a bumbling teenager. "There's going to be a live band and dancing," I say, then wince at how lame that sounds. I should be complimenting her on that gorgeous dress or how amazing she looks with her hair up in that fancy style.

Libby takes my hand and squeezes it. "Hopefully I don't trip on these high heels," she says with a laugh.

"Right now, with such a beautiful woman on my arm, I think I could trip over my own two feet. And they're on solid ground. Or, solid car floor at least." Another cringe-inducing comment on my part slips out of my lips, but Libby doesn't seem to notice.

I keep my mouth shut for the rest of the ride, soaking in the soft music, luxurious interior, and beautiful woman beside me. Libby doesn't seem to notice the silence as she takes inventory of the limo's interior by opening and closing a few of the many compartments. When she reveals the liquor cabinet, she arches an eyebrow but doesn't comment. Some of our guests, especially the sports agents, enjoy a stiff drink, although I rarely partake.

She turns a knob, and the music abruptly changes from soft jazz to hard rock, but she flinches and quickly switches it back. When she fiddles with the lighting control, the interior turns a neon blue color.

"Oops! Now we look like smurfs," she says, and we both laugh.

"I've never been to one of these fancy, schmancy events. I avoided them at all costs when Griff had to attend these things and needed a plus one, but I think I was missing out," Libby says in an awestruck voice as the limo draws up under the hotel's porte-cochere. Bright lights twinkle around us as we exit the car. A bellman opens the shiny brass doors and we're swooshed inside when the air pressure sucks us in. I put my arm around Libby, and we walk towards the glitzy ballroom. With her nestled against me, I feel like the prince with Cinderella on my arm.

This no longer feels like a fake date. It's becoming very real.

Sixteen – The Charming Mr. Bigshot

Libby

The hotel lights sparkle, and I feel like a celebrity as we exit the limo. Fortunately no paparazzi are hanging around the entrance, but a few hotel guests gawk at us as we walk inside. I overhear one lady comment to her friend, "Do you recognize those two? I think the man is an actor. Didn't he star in that action comedy with Sandra Bullock last year?"

Brent looks hunky in his well-fitting black tux, but I'm not sure he resembles Channing Tatum. Though when he puts his arm around me, I truly feel like Cinderella at the ball with my Prince Charming.

Conversations swirl as we walk into the crowded ballroom, overflowing with people who are wearing their finest and are not afraid to show off their wealth. Diamonds, couture gowns, and tuxes fill the room, along with the sounds of waiters preparing to serve dinner. Utensils clank. Someone laughs. A noisy cart loaded with plates rolls by, the vibrating front wheel squeaking under the weight.

I soak in the glamour surrounding me, not sure that I'll ever have an opportunity to come to one of these high-end events again. The ballroom literally sparkles, from the giant crystal chandelier hanging overhead, to the polished granite floors under our feet, to each table's dazzling gold and silver centerpieces.

"Brent! I'm so glad you came," an older woman in a long gold lamé dress says as she approaches. A pair of reading glasses dangles from her neck. She's reed thin and stands well over six-feet tall in those heels. When she strides up beside my date, he's a few inches shorter than she is.

Brent and the woman exchange hugs as I hover in the background. They obviously know each other well.

"I expect you and your father to open your wallets tonight," she says in a firm, no-nonsense, teacherlike voice.

Brent nods and chuckles at her blatant request. "Eleanor, this is Libby Griffin, my date," Brent says, pulling me forward for introductions. "Eleanor is the head of the charity we're supporting this evening."

"Nice to meet you," I murmur. *Am I supposed to shake her hand or curtsy?*

Eleanor gives me a thorough appraisal. Her scrutiny is rather discomforting, and I wonder if I'll pass muster. After several ticks, she squeezes Brent's arm. "This one is much better than your last few. At least she's wearing clothes," Eleanor states with a finely arched eyebrow.

Brent and I exchange amused looks as the woman strides off, yelling someone else's name.

"Sorry. Eleanor's a bit like a bull in a china shop, but she means well," Brent says after she's out of earshot.

I chuckle. No wonder this charity gala is so successful. With a woman like Eleanor at the helm, no one could dare to not "open their wallet."

"Parents approaching," Brent mutters right before we're accosted by the flamboyant pair. Brent's mom is wearing a yellow flowy evening gown that swirls around her ankles as she walks, and his dad is clad in a black tuxedo with a neon yellow bow tie, I guess as a nod to the mom's dress color. I suddenly feel a bit underdressed with my exposed shoulder and short hemline.

"Brent and Libby! Don't you both look stunning! You make such a cute couple together," Brent's mom enthuses as she yanks me into a bear hug that literally takes my breath away and almost topples me off my high heels. "What a gorgeous dress! Modest yet eye-catching," she adds with a wink. My heart sinks as I think about how I'm only here because Brent's normal dates are unacceptable to his parents.

Brent and his dad do the male version of hugging, with lots of backslaps. Mrs. Masterson gives Brent an equally enthusiastic hug as she gave me. I catch her saying something about his date and dress fabric. Somewhere during this whirlwind process, I manage to shake Mr. Masterson's hand.

"We're sitting over there," Brent's mom says, pointing to a table near the center of the room. "It's table number seven. We'll meet you there in a few," she adds, tugging on Mr. Masterson's hand. "I see Eleanor over by the beverage bar." They disappear as quickly as they arrived.

I catch my breath and give Brent a playful grin. "Whew! Another force of nature," I say.

Brent chuckles. "Kind of like your roommate."

I arch an eyebrow, wondering what Maggie did while I wasn't in the room. She acts like a mother hen sometimes.

We slowly make our way towards table seven, stopping every few feet to speak to people along the way. A profusion of sports agents stop Brent trying to peddle one of their soon-to-be unemployed clients. Brent politely takes their business card and says he'll get back to them. My date has particularly warm words for an elderly couple who have season tickets. And he shares high fives with athletes clad in outlandish trendy tuxes—one of which is purple with lavender stripes—all with glimmering models hanging off their arms. Blinking at all the wild colors and barely-there dresses, I suddenly feel like my dress is rather conservative. But I'd never be able to pull off some of these outfits.

I didn't realize that Brent knows so many people, of all generations and walks of life. He's really well-connected, and all of them are excited to see him. They wave or grab his arm to catch his attention. I patiently hover at his side, and he gallantly introduces me to every group, a warmth spreading through me as to how proud he seems to be that I'm his date. I have to keep reminding myself that he's just acting for his parents' sake. Several of the older ladies comment on how much material is in my dress. *What exactly did his previous dates wear?*

Brent's popularity and ability to schmooze with the best of them has me tongue-tied. I teasingly called him Mr. Bigshot in the past, but he really is a bigshot.

Sam Hudson, wearing a cranberry-colored tux, strolls up and immediately starts flirting with me, his shameless disregard of my date standing beside me setting my teeth on edge. *Does this guy really think I'd flirt with him while on a date with Brent?*

"Libby! Don't you look gorgeous," Sam says, pulling me into a hug as if we're best friends. I give him a quick pat on the back and quickly disengage from the hug. Brent gives me a sour look while Sam's agent, Adam, chats about the news coverage of Sam's contract extension. Adam bends Brent's ear, bragging about the amount of airtime spent discussing the extension, as if that makes his client even more valuable.

I return to Brent's side, and he puts his arm around my waist, giving Sam one of his patented glares. It's an overt "she's mine" move, and butterflies flare in my stomach. The action takes me a bit by surprise since this is a fake date, but I must say the gesture makes it look like we're dating for real.

"We need to get over to our table. Please pardon us, gentlemen," Brent says, gently spurring me on.

"You two were sure cozy," Brent mutters as we stride away, his male pride obviously stinging from the encounter.

"I haven't seen Sam since the contract meeting," I say to mollify the prick of jealousy in Brent's voice. Belatedly I wonder why Sam doesn't have a date on his arm.

Brent blows out a loud breath. "Sorry! I shouldn't stand in the way if you want to date him. My bad."

I put a hand on Brent's forearm, feeling the steely muscles tighten under my fingertips. "Brent, I wouldn't date Sam in a million years. Plus, I'm fake dating you at the moment!" I add in a teasing voice.

Brent gives me an indecipherable look. "Right. We need to put on a good show for the parents."

That look and his comment send my mind racing. Could he possibly wish we weren't fake dating? Was all the pride in his voice and the possessive gesture genuine? My heart flips at the thought.

~*~

After the delicious meal of salmon or steak (I had salmon) along with some yummy fingerling potatoes in a divine cheese sauce (I snagged a few off Brent's plate while he wasn't looking), one of Brent's mom's friends, Mrs. Feldman, talks my ear off about the health benefits of hot yoga.

"You simply must try it," she says. "It's life changing. You sweat out all the toxins in your body while at the same time building core muscles!"

Any sentence with sweat and muscles in it I want nothing to do with. Brent's shoulders shake with suppressed laughter as he squeezes my knee under the table.

"I'm pretty busy right now, what with working for this guy," I say, playfully pointing to Brent.

The woman cackles. "I bet you are, dear," she says, waggling her eyebrows.

I ignore that implication. "I also just adopted a puppy. We walk to the dog park every day," I feel compelled to add this tidbit in case the woman keeps twisting my arm. I can point to walking—in my case more like strolling—as a form of exercise.

Thankfully the woman turns to Brent's mom and engages her in a discussion about joining a bowling league.

I chuckle. *Hot yoga? Bowling? I wonder what's next? Archery, perhaps?*

"Mrs. Feldman can be a bit much," Brent whispers, his breath sending goosebumps across my neck. I didn't realize he was this close. "How about we dance before you get recruited for the bowling league?"

I'd fake a hamstring pull before getting recruited for a bowling league. "Dancing sounds fun," I say, taking the hand Brent extends to me. He tugs me to my feet and we join several couples on the dance floor. Fortunately, the song is a slow one. Brent and I sway back and forth to the music, emulating most of the other couples. One overachieving pair floats by doing the waltz with perfectly choreographed steps.

"I apologize now if I step on your toes," Brent says, pulling me even closer. I relax and place my head on his solid chest, the steady thump of his heart under my ear. Since The Rules aren't in play for an off-hours function, I can ignore them and enjoy breaking each one.

"We're barely moving, so I doubt you'll step on anything," I tease. A tinge of remorse hits knowing that I could have had a magical evening like this with Brent all those years ago. *Is it finally time to hear Brent's side of The Debacle?*

He nods towards the Ginger Rogers and Fred Astaire wannabes. "I've never been much of a dancer."

Gazing up at him, I say, "I flunked out of ballet when I was six, so I never returned for any more lessons—even when we were in high school and Grams insisted Griff learn how to waltz and wanted me to come along."

I feel Brent's chuckle under my ear. "Sounds like we're quite the pair. How does one flunk out of ballet class exactly?"

Blushing slightly, the truth tumbles unchecked from my lips. "I was attempting an arabesque," I say, vividly remembering the moment. Brent's confused look makes me add, "That's where you stand on one leg with a slight bend in your knee, while the other leg is extended straight behind and at a right angle."

He grimaces. "That sounds tricky. Were you wearing a tutu?" he asks, waggling his eyebrows.

I giggle and smack his arm. "Yes, a bright pink one, along with white tights. It was quite the sight."

He smirks. "Well, what happened? Did you kick someone with your extended leg?"

"I toppled over into Suzy Warner, taking her out along with the girl beside her. We all landed in a heap of pink tulle. Suzy's mom accused me of being a clumsy oaf, so I never went back."

"That's awful! You were only six," Brent huffs.

I grin at his indignation over Mrs. Warner's unkind words. "Mom made me feel better with a trip to the ice cream parlor. Honestly, I was never going to excel at ballet, so it was kind of a blessing in disguise." A pang hits knowing this is one of the few remaining clear memories I have of my mom.

"I still feel sad for your six-year-old self," Brent says, gently tucking me back under his chin.

We sway in silence, the kind that feels comfortable and not awkward. The band stops playing when Eleanor strides to the front of the room and grabs a microphone. "If you haven't bid on the silent auction items, do so now because we're closing the auction in five minutes!"

There's a mad scramble to the auction table where all the items are on display, so Brent and I remain on the dance floor, hoping to avoid a collision with anyone.

"Did you want to bid on the gym membership?" Brent asks with a straight face.

I elbow him in the ribs. "Are you kidding?!"

"How about the golf outing with the team's stadium announcer?"

My nose wrinkles at the mention of the loud baseball call-by-call guy. "He talks too much, and I don't know how to play golf."

Brent grins. "Ah, you're eyeing the concert tickets to The Smashing Pumpkins, aren't you?"

I raise an eyebrow. "No, but I saw you gazing at that giant fruit basket. Do you want to get your bid in?"

The fruit basket has been the talk of the event, because it's become a game to try to identify all the different types of fruit neatly stacked in the humongous container. The layers of pink and green cellophane wrapper add to the intrigue.

Brent laughs and tugs me back towards our table. I give a sigh of relief when I spot Mrs. Feldman clear across the room bidding on the catered BBQ picnic, complete with a bouncy house. *Whew!* She's too far away for any more weird sporting activities recruitment talk. Though instead of stopping at our table, Brent walks on by.

"That was our table—" I point behind as he propels me through the room and onto the balcony. With the excitement over the silent auction, we're out here alone. It's a relief to get out of the loud ballroom for a bit.

"What a sight!" I exclaim as the twinkling cityscape unfurls before us. We're high enough to see for miles.

Brent stands beside me at the railing as we soak in the view. After a few seconds, he turns me to face him. "Are you having a good time?" he asks.

I nod, too mesmerized by his eyes to form an intelligent sentence. His thumb makes a slow circle on my exposed shoulder, causing goosebumps on my arms and neck. Our eyes lock and I feel like the center of his world. I don't dare blink, wishing this moment would last forever.

"That dress is spectacular," he murmurs. Brent leans towards me as if in slow motion, and my heart goes into overdrive. He gives me plenty of time to pull back, but I don't. Those blasted rules float into my mind, but I shove them away. *No rules while fake dating!*

Our lips meet, pressing softly together at first, stealing my ability to breathe. Brent runs his hands down my back until they rest on my waist, holding me steady for the kiss. Luckily my high heels elevate me enough that I don't need to stand on my tiptoes.

I wrap my arms around his neck, and our kiss goes on and on, for an instant or an eternity, I'm not sure which. The pent-up attraction between us explodes like a wildfire. He kisses me like he means it, and this fake date suddenly goes from phony to very real.

"Did you see the look on the lady's face who won that fruit basket? She looked like she won the lottery." The voices make us jump and Brent pulls back, separating our lips. I squint over his shoulder at the noisy group who broke up the best moment of my life. A toe-curling, perfect kiss like no other I've ever had before.

Resting his forehead on mine, Brent says with a contrite sigh, "We probably should go back inside, or Mom will come looking for us."

Bummer. No more kisses? "Okay," I say trying to hide the disappointment on my face.

He steers me gently back into the ballroom where we join his parents at our table. His mom bid on the same BBQ picnic as Mrs. Feldman, so there's quite a verbal sparring match between them before the winner is announced, each proclaiming they got the last bid in. Both women groan loudly when a ninety-year-old man wins the prize.

"What does he need a bouncy house for?" Mrs. Feldman mutters.

After that, the evening ends far too quickly. Unfortunately, there's no repeat performance of The Kiss because Mr. and Mrs. Masterson catch a ride with us in the limo. When we get to my apartment, Brent walks me to my door, giving me a rueful look. His mom has her face plastered to the passenger side window, curtailing any lingering goodnight scene.

"I had a wonderful time, Libby," he says, then gives me a gentlemanly peck on the cheek and hustles back to the car.

Floating into my apartment, I'm happy when Maggie is nowhere in sight. I just want to bask in The Kiss and not have to answer all her questions.

I fall asleep with a lovestruck smile on my face after kissing my Prince Charming. The smile fades as one last thought hits before I fall asleep. Cinderella had a magical time at the ball, but was it real?

Seventeen – The Debacle Part 1

Brent

After that megawatt kiss, I don't sleep a wink. I tossed and turned all night, wrestling with the fact that I've fallen for Libby. This fake dating plan is suddenly no longer fake. *At least not for me.* But what about Libby? I felt like she was having a good time with me, but maybe she's just a fantastic actress. I do remember her frightening ability to tell a convincing lie when we were kids.

When Libby arrives at the office the next morning, we avoid each other for the first hour. She stays at her desk, working quietly while I sit at my desk and stew. I can't concentrate on business as I mull over the developing relationship with my assistant.

This subdued version of Libby is unfamiliar. It's like I'm walking down a path and don't know whether it's going to be a minefield or as smooth as ice. Is she feeling the same way I do or is she regretting our impulsive kiss? I refuse to apologize for violating one of her rules. We both fully participated in that mind-numbing kiss. She can't deny that.

Deciding that if we have any chance to move forward to an authentic relationship—and I desperately want that—I've got to explain the prom night debacle in hopes that she'll finally forgive me. Or at least understand my side of what happened.

"Libby, can you come in here for a minute?" I yell, barricaded behind my desk, keeping the wooden surface as a buffer between me and Libby. I need to get this story out and not be tempted to kiss her.

She peeks her head in my office, hesitating beside the doorframe, a look of nervousness on her face. "What do you need, Mr. Masterson?"

Her formality throws me off. *Maybe she didn't enjoy that kiss as much as I did?*

113

"Please sit down," I say, waving my hand towards the chairs positioned in front of my desk.

She avoids making eye contact as she sits down, staring instead at the notebook and pen clasped in her hand.

"I want to explain what happened on prom night. You need to understand my side of the story."

Her eyes fly to mine. "That's not necessary! I was there, remember?"

Groaning, I pinch the bridge of my nose. "Please? I want to give you my perspective."

She purses her lips and scowls, then shrugs. "Fine. Go ahead."

Her reaction isn't encouraging, but I plow ahead with the story . . .

~*~

Eight Years Ago

I'm a bundle of nerves as the clock ticks towards the time I'm supposed to pick up my prom date. It'll be a miracle if I manage not to sweat through my fancy shirt. I've been dressed in the rented tux and shirt for over an hour.

My emotions are all over the place, bouncing between dread and excitement. Griff's warnings about dating his sister ring ominously inside my head. Griff confronted me outside my locker the day after I asked Libby to the dance.

"What are you doing, man?" he hissed between gritted teeth.

I pointed to my locker. "Getting my history textbook?"

"No, not that. Asking Libby to the prom. That's a dumb idea. Really dumb!"

Uh-oh. I never mentioned my plan to Griff, but I didn't think I had to.

114

"You don't date your best friend's sister," he growls. "She's off limits."

"Why?" I fired back.

"What happens when you break up? I'll be caught in the middle." He stormed off without another word, but I've agonized over his warning ever since. I almost called off the date a couple times, but then I'd see Libby in the hall and be reminded as to why I asked her out. Griff cooled off after a couple days, but he never got behind the idea of me taking Libby to the prom.

Pacing in my bedroom, I wait, kicking myself for getting ready too soon. I still have fifty-three minutes until I steer Mom and Dad's boat-sized Buick one driveway over to pick up my date. Considering that's a fifteen-second drive at most, I've really jumped the gun on putting on my tux.

"Brent, I need your help," Mom yells from the bottom of the stairway.

Cringing at this unexpected request, I walk to the top of the stairs. "What do you need, Mom?"

Her eyes widen. "You're dressed already?" She glances at the living room clock. "Isn't there almost an hour before you are supposed to pick Libby up?"

Fifty-two minutes now, to be precise.

I flush, my enthusiasm and nervousness towards this date probably apparent from my neatly combed hair to the polished shoes on my feet. "I didn't want to be late," I say lamely.

Mom grins. "Well, considering we live next door to her, I don't think there's much chance of that."

But it's me, I want to say. Murphy always seems to raise his ugly head at the most inopportune times. Like when bases were loaded and a 10-mph pitch hit me in the head in Little League, knocking me out.

"Grandma Laverne has a flat tire and AAA can't come for two hours. We need to go rescue her," Mom says with apology lacing her voice. "I'd go by myself, but . . ." Since Mom threw out her back last year, she's not supposed to lift anything over twenty pounds.

Pointing to my outfit, I say, "I shouldn't go like this."

"Go change. You'll have plenty of time to get dressed again when we get back."

Grandma Laverne lives five minutes away. I calculate the time to drive there, change a tire (maybe fifteen minutes?), and drive back. Twenty-five minutes seems like it would be cutting it too close for a wardrobe change.

"I'll wear this. Let's go!" I say as I bound down the stairs.

Mom grabs her purse, muttering something about my inappropriate clothing, and follows me out to the garage. I back the massive Buick out and head to my grandmother's house. As I pass by Libby's house, I glance at her bedroom window, wondering whether she's dressed already and is as anxious about this date as I am. *Did Griff try to talk her out of it?*

"Your father would have a fit if we didn't help. You know how he is since Granddad died, like an overgrown watchdog."

"I know, Mom. It's just bad timing," I say with a sigh.

"Don't worry, son. You'll have that tire fixed in a jiffy."

As we pull up, I see Grandmother's massive Lincoln Town Car sitting in her driveway like a beached whale, leaning to the side. The rear driver's side tire is flat as a pancake.

I park at the curb and Mom jumps out right as Grandma strides from inside the front door, dressed like she's going to church. She looks rather overdressed for volunteering at the Sunnydale Nursing Center, but her Southern roots won't let her leave the house in anything but church-appropriate attire.

"Thank goodness you're here! I'm supposed to help serve dinner and dessert, then read Mr. Henderson his favorite book. But

I'm so sorry to put you out." Grandma's distraught expression does me in. She looks forward to volunteering at the nursing home. It's the highlight of her week.

"No worries. I'll get the tire fixed in a few minutes," I say with more confidence than I'm feeling. *When was the last time I changed a tire? Maybe never.*

Grandma pauses, taking in my attire. "Why are you dressed in that monkey suit, Brent?"

I shuffle my feet. "Um, this is what I'm wearing to prom."

"Goodness gracious. Is this going to make you late?" Grandma's look of concern is genuine.

"We're fine, Laverne. He doesn't have to leave for an hour," Mom chimes in.

Grandma nods. "So why did you come to fix a flat tire wearing that?" she says, surprise lacing her voice.

Mom steps in. "He's nervous as a cat in a room full of rocking chairs over his first date with the neighbor girl." Grandma and Mom trade grins and a few giggles.

"Well, isn't that sweet," Grandma says.

I frown as the seconds are still ticking by. "Where's your keys? I need to open the trunk," I say using my grumpiest voice, wanting to move this show along.

Grandma hands me the keys and I rummage through the trunk, looking for the spare tire and the tools to change it. The tux jacket is rather constrictive, so I remove it and hand it to Mom.

The ladies watch as I wrestle the tire from the trunk. This isn't one of those weeny small spare tires, it's a full-sized one. I grapple with it for several seconds and feel it rubbing against my chest before it clears the surprisingly deep well of the trunk. These Town Cars sure have a roomy rear storage space—you can probably haul ten suitcases in this thing.

"Brent, be careful, you've dirtied your shirt," Mom says pointing to a black smudge running along the front of my neatly pressed shirt. I tell myself not to fret, I'll just change into another shirt when I get back home. I can whip this one off and put on another one in less than a minute in case we're running a bit late.

"Do you have something I can put down on the ground so I don't get my pants dirty?" My belated request comes after I notice a grease stain on the driveway right beside where I need to kneel.

"Oh, yes! Let me go get something," Grandma says, then bustles off to the house. I glance at my wristwatch (which I probably should also remove). *Yikes!* My heart rate accelerates. I've already used up fifteen minutes of the allotted twenty-five minutes to get this job done.

"Here you go," Grandma says, handing me a ratty blanket. Despite its dubious condition, it looks clean.

Kneeling on the blanket, I put the jack under the Lincoln and crank . . . and crank . . . and crank. After what feels like hours, the heavy car is finally high enough to remove the old tire and put on the new one. But I'm severely out of breath and sweating.

Taking the lug wrench, I remove three lug nuts with speed and ease. The fourth one won't budge. It's as if the nut is welded firmly in place. Grunting and straining my seventeen-year-old scrawny, under-developed muscles, I twist the tool over and over to no avail.

"Put your whole body into it," Grandma suggests.

"You can't get any leverage kneeling," Mom adds.

I scowl at the helpful advice from the ladies, then leap to my feet. Grabbing the lug wrench again, I bend over and push on the tool for all I'm worth, putting my whole body into the motion.

Riiiip!

I nearly fall to the ground when the nut releases.

Why does my backside suddenly feel exposed?

118

Running my hand over the seam of my pants, my worst fear is realized. I've split the tuxedo pants right up the back seam. Craning my neck to look at the damage, the large gaping hole exposes my white underwear for all to see.

Grandma and Mom gasp. "Oh dear," Grandma murmurs.

I ignore the rip and continue with my task. Nothing to be done about it now. I have some slacks from the last charity event my dad dragged me to, I think. As I remove the old tire and put on the new one, Mom says, "I can sew those up in no time when we get home."

Her comment doesn't make me feel any better, as several more minutes have ticked off the clock, making my twenty-five minutes of allocated time to change the tire and get back home a pipe dream at this point. We'll be lucky if there's five minutes of buffer to pick up Libby by the time we get back. *Maybe it's a sign. Maybe Griff was right.*

Libby's pretty face pops into my mind and I shake the foreboding thought away. Picking up the pace, I pull off the old tire and put on the new one. In my haste, I kick two of the lug nuts underneath the car. Bending, I see them just out of arm's reach. Suppressing a frustrated growl, I get on my stomach and shimmy under the behemoth Lincoln, retrieving the nuts. When I pop back out from under the vehicle, I see another black smudge on my shirt as well as on the front of my pants.

"A quick spritz of water and a lint brush will get that stain out of your pants," Mom declares in an upbeat voice. "But you will need to change that shirt, dear."

Pushing aside thoughts of my now filthy, ruined tuxedo and shirt, I tighten the last two nuts, crank the jack down, and return all tools to the trunk. The Lincoln no longer tilts to the side, although the spare tire looks a bit under inflated.

"Don't you need to add a little air?" Grandma asks, surveying the new tire.

"Do you have a pump?" I shoot back.

Her expression becomes thoughtful, and she wrings her hands. "Why don't you just go on and I'll ask a neighbor to pump it up for me? I don't want you to be late."

Dad's stern face pops into my head and my shoulders straighten. "We came here to get your car fully functioning. Is there a pump I can borrow?"

Grandma taps her chin. "I think Bob across the street has one."

Visions of getting to Libby's house thirty minutes late flood my mind. I take off at a full run to the neighbor's house. I must look like an idiot—a guy in a black tuxedo, his white underwear hanging out the back seam, sprinting down the street.

"Can I help ya?" Bob says, staring at me through the screen door like I'm an escaped felon.

Huffing and puffing for air, I wheeze, "I'm Laverne's . . . grandson . . . Do you . . . have a . . . tire pump?" At the end of that winded sentence, I bend over, put my hands on my knees and suck in more air.

When did I get so out of shape? Oh, yeah, when I quit running track in favor of the debate team.

"Let me go check. Meet ya at the garage."

He disappears while I get my heart rate back to normal. The garage door slowly raises, and Bob appears holding a tire pump.

"Thanks!" I say, swiping the pump from his hand and sprinting back down the street.

"Your pants are split!" Bob yells at my retreating back loud enough for the entire neighborhood to hear.

I raise my hand in acknowledgement but keep on running. Winded again when I get back to the Lincoln, I slump against the trunk, trying to regain control of my breathing.

"Give me the pump, son," Mom says.

"What about your back?" I ask.

"Pumping isn't lifting," Mom says with a dismissive hand wave.

My eyes widen, but I don't complain and hand her the pump. She attaches it to the tire and pumps furiously. In less than thirty seconds, the tire looks like new. I view Mom in a new, more impressed light. She sure can pump up a tire in a pinch.

"Okay Laverne, looks like your wheels are back in running order," Mom says, dusting her hands off.

Grandma smiles. "Thank you so much! The Sunnyvale residents also thank you. They look so forward to my apple pie." She nods towards the backseat where a considerable number of pies are carefully stacked inside cardboard boxes. I hadn't even noticed them until now.

She climbs into the monstrosity, rolls her window down and waves. "Thank you! Brent, I know your prom will be great. No one is on time to those kinds of things anyway." The car rolls slowly down the street. Thankfully I got the lug nuts tight enough and the tire doesn't fall off.

My heart plummets after Grandma's comment. How long have we been here? A glance at my watch confirms that I'm almost forty minutes late to pick up Libby. We still have to return the tire pump to Bob, Mom needs to stitch up my pants, and I need to change into a new shirt. Maybe also apply some additional deodorant after all the sweating.

"I guess we shouldn't have come to change the tire. I never thought it would take so long," Mom bemoans after I run the tire pump back to Bob.

I frown but bite my tongue. In the haste to get Grandma to the nursing home on time, I never thought to contact Libby. Slumping in the driver's seat of Mom's car, I tap out a text to Libby. My fingers fly on the tiny keyboard as I type, retype, and re-retype the message, undecided as to what to do. Should I let her know I'm going to be late, or should I just cancel?

All the calamities that happened over the last hour and a half roll through my head.

Ripping my tuxedo pants.

Soiling my shirt.

Losing the lug nuts under the car.

Is the universe trying to tell me something? Am I not supposed to date my best friend's sister? Griff's warning, the ticking clock, and my filthy outfit and torn pants send me over the edge.

Me: Something came up and I won't be able to make prom. Sorry.

The words look lame and inadequate, but I hit send before I can rethink the situation. I feel horrible about not breaking off the date with Libby sooner. She's going to hate me after this. But maybe that's best. Dating Griff's sister was a dumb idea.

"Getting to the prom a little late won't matter, you'll just miss a few dances. I'm sure Libby will understand once you explain everything," Mom says in an optimistic tone as we drive back home.

"It won't matter now. I just cancelled the date," I reply in a flat voice.

"What!?" Mom's eyes go round. "I'll help you repair your pants and there's another ironed shirt in your closet." The urgency in her voice says she'll do everything in her power to help me get ready again.

"Griff said I shouldn't date her," I say quietly. "He was pretty mad about it."

A sympathetic expression crosses Mom's face. "No wonder you've been down in the dumps lately. You feel like you have to choose between your best friend and his sister?"

I nod.

"Not an easy choice," Mom adds.

I shake my head. "It isn't. Libby will be mad at me for a few days, that's all."

Deciding to go home and lick my wounds, I put the car in gear and head back home.

I hide in my room for the rest of the weekend, knowing in my heart that Libby won't be mad for just a few days. She'll never give me a chance again.

When I see Libby in the hall on Monday, she won't even look at me. I'm hovering beside my locker when Griff strides up and smacks me on the arm.

"You cancelled the date with Libby at the last minute? What were you thinking, man?" His voice rises with every word.

I take a step back. "I thought you would be happy! What about me not dating your sister? I didn't date her," I huff.

Griff rolls his eyes. "This isn't what I had in mind. Why'd you really back out?"

I don't admit that his warning played a big part in me deciding to cancel, instead I say, "Grandma had an emergency and I got delayed. I figured it was best just to bow out at that point rather than arrive late." *And feed the high school gossip train.*

He glares at me. "Well, you don't have to worry about dating my sister ever again. She may never speak to you."

My shoulders slump. "I know."

His anger loses steam. "Let's forget this whole debacle. I'll see you at baseball practice this afternoon." He strides off, leaving me feeling worse than I already did.

I've managed to crater any potential relationship with Libby and ruin my friendship with Griff in one fell swoop. Regret eats at my gut for the remainder of the school year.

~*~

Although my friendship with Griff eventually got back on more solid ground, that debacle hung over my head for years. My eyes land on Libby after re-telling the flat tire fiasco that ruined my chances with her all those years ago. She's not scowling any longer, which I take as a positive sign.

"Did Griff really get mad when you asked me out?"

I nod. "Yep. He was pretty clear about his feelings." I still feel the sting of his words to this day.

She chews on her lower lip, blinking back what looks like tears. "May I tell my side of the story now?" she asks quietly.

I want to leap over the desk, haul her into my arms, plant another kiss on her lips, and beg for her to give us another chance. But I'm emotionally wrung out over the re-telling, so instead I merely slump in my seat. "Go ahead."

Eighteen – The Debacle Part 2

Libby

After hearing Brent's side of the story, I berate myself for not asking for an explanation years ago. What a fool I was! But what fifteen-year-old girl uses sound logic after she thought she was being callously stood up? And on the biggest night of her life.

All I could think about was the fact that I never got to wear that beautiful dress Grams bought me. The price was way over the agreed-to budget, but she bought it for me anyway.

Why did Griff get involved? He's always been a protective big brother, but I never knew he didn't want me to date Brent. This explains a lot of things, like Griff's comment after the prom that Brent cancelling was probably for the best. At the time I just thought Griff was trying to make me feel better. There's also the conversation Griff and I had about me working for Brent. Griff advised against that, too. If—and it's a big if—I ever actually dated Brent, would Griff stand in the way?

Blinking back tears, I look at Brent. His anxious expression tells me that he wants me to forgive him. Truth is, I forgave him about halfway through his heart-touching story. *How can I stay mad at a guy who jeopardized his prom date to help his grandmother?*

But I want him to understand my side of things as well and why I acted so—what now seems—unreasonable. At the time, freezing him out felt like the right thing to do; pay back the clod who cancelled our date at the last minute. "May I tell my side of the story now?"

His face drops. "Go ahead," he says, in a flat tone.

The fact that I didn't leap to my feet, run around the desk, and haul him into an "I forgive you" kiss has disappointed him greatly. I almost ditch my plan to tell my story in light of his dejected expression. Instead, I steel my emotions and launch into my side of the debacle . . .

~*~

Eight Years Ago

The plastic garment bag hangs on the door to my closet. I keep looking at it and pinching myself that I get to wear the gorgeous blue dress in a couple hours. I'm also feeling on cloud nine that the boy next door, who I've crushed on for years, is my date. This night is going to be magical—a dream come true.

"Sandy's here to fix your hair," Grams yells from the bottom of the stairs. My sweet grandmother hired her hairdresser to come to our house and fix my hair, citing that an unexpected windstorm could ruin the look before we got home from the salon.

I tromp down the stairs, taking them two at a time. Grams and Sandy gasp as they watch me stumble and nearly break my neck.

"Don't fall! You won't be able to dance with Brent if you do that," Grams warns.

I slow down and carefully take the last few steps.

Sandy sets up shop at the dining room table, laying out all her hair styling tools. I pull a photo I clipped from a magazine from my jeans pocket and hand it to her. "I want my hair to look like this."

She stares closely at the photo and nods. Sandy's a wizard with hair, so I trust she'll be able to achieve the look. After she shampoos my hair at the laundry room sink in a lovely shampoo that smells like vanilla and coconut, I sit with one of those plastic capes draped around me in a dining table chair and Sandy starts to work her magic.

Sandy and Grams chat as I close my eyes and enjoy the hair massage while Sandy dries, curls, and twists my hair into the complicated style. She uses a raft of bobby pins and some styling gel to wrangle my usually unruly locks into position. I wonder whether my hair style can withstand the dance moves I plan to do with Brent. I've been practicing for weeks, looking in my bedroom mirror to ensure I've perfected the steps to look exactly like the dancers I see on YouTube.

About an hour later, Sandy stands back with a smile. "There! That should do it." She hands me a mirror and I gasp. The girl staring back at me looks nothing like little Libby Griffin. I look grown-up and possibly even pretty.

Hopefully Brent will think so.

"You look gorgeous, Libby!" Grams enthuses. Thankfully Griff and Gramps are nowhere about because I'm sure they'd say something awkward to distract from the moment. Grams banned them from the house until after I'm fully dressed, and I'm so grateful.

Once Sandy has packed up and left, Grams follows me upstairs. She's going to give me some makeup tips and help me get into my dress.

Sitting on the edge of my bed while I remove my newly purchased packages of mascara, eye shadow, and lip gloss from a dresser drawer, Grams says in a quiet voice, "You look so much like your mother. It's remarkable."

My eyes widen, my memories of Mom a bit fuzzy since she and Dad died when I was in fourth grade. That's when Grams and Gramps took us in.

"You think so?" I ask staring into the mirror above my dresser. I want to get out the photo of Mom that I have tucked away in one of the drawers and compare myself to it, but I resist.

"Yes. You remind me of your father too. A bit impulsive and flighty at times, but you're the spitting image of your mom."

I don't take offense to Grams' backhanded compliment because even as a teenager, I recognize that I'm impulsive and flighty. I grab a tissue, suppressing a sniffle and wiping away a few tears produced by the memories of my parents. A glance over my shoulder shows Grams blinking back a few tears as well.

Grams coaches me on my makeup application as I apply too much eye shadow and have to wipe it off and start over. Twice. My hands shake from nerves when I try to put on the mascara. Taking several calming breaths, I steady my right hand with my left and manage to apply the black eyelash enhancer without giving myself racoon eyes.

I glance at the One Direction clock on my bedroom wall—the one I just had to have because of my middle school crush on Harry Styles. The gaudy clock seems a little lame now to my more mature self, but I can't part with it. My heart rate ticks up because Brent will be here in just fifteen minutes.

I bustle over to the closet and retrieve the dress still hanging in its protective plastic. Slowly I pull off the plastic and gasp in delight when I see the dress again.

"That one is much better than my choice," Grams admits with a chuckle.

Her choice was an ugly pink pleated maxi dress with poofy sleeves and a ruffle running around the hemline. I looked like . . . well, someone from Grams' era. Thankfully the store clerk agreed with me and lobbied for the blue dress as hard as I did.

Grams zips down the back zipper and I step into the dress. Once the zipper is closed, I look in the mirror. The dress fits me like a glove, and with my new hairstyle and makeup, I could pass for a sophisticated eighteen-year-old.

Blinking back more tears, Grams says, "Libby you are beautiful. Let's go down and show Gramps."

"Your young man is going to faint when he sees you," Gramps comments when I make my appearance downstairs. In five minutes, Brent will be pulling into the driveway, and I can't wait.

Butterflies flutter in my stomach, and I'm grateful that I skipped lunch—otherwise it might make an unwelcome re-appearance.

Griff has already dressed and left to pick up his date, so my date should be here any second.

I nervously pace the living room, back and forth from the east wall to the west wall, peeking every two seconds out the front window, wondering where Brent is. The living room clock taunts me as it loudly ticks off the minutes that Brent hasn't arrived.

Tick. Tick. Tick.

I want to yank the clock off the wall and toss it in the trash.

Tick. Tick. Tick.

He's now five minutes late.

"He'll be here any minute. Maybe he popped a button on his shirt or spilled toothpaste on his tie," Gramps suggests.

When Brent is ten minutes late, I sag down onto the sofa. My feet hurt from all this pacing, plus I'm probably wearing out Grams' twelve-year-old carpet. A few wrinkles on my dress beats having my feet ache.

Twenty minutes late . . .

Gramps and Grams talk quietly in the corner, and I catch a few words. Something about one of them running over to the Mastersons' house to check whether everyone is okay.

Forty minutes late . . .

The sympathetic looks coming from my grandparents make me want to scream. Either that or burst into tears.

Did I misunderstand the time he's coming?

The dance has already started, and we've missed the hard-as-rocks cookies and the punch that a group of juniors plan to spike. Principal Henderson announced on the school PA system on Friday that he's doing his hip hop moves and that those shouldn't be missed. I cringe thinking about how tongues will wag when Brent and I walk in this late.

Ping!

My cell chimes and I sag with relief when I see it's from Brent. After I read and reread the text, my heart shatters into a million pieces.

Brent: Something came up and I won't be able to make prom. Sorry.

I leap to my feet and run upstairs. Too embarrassed, humiliated, and mortified to say anything to Grams and Gramps.

Grams comes up and tries to talk to me through my closed bedroom door, but I turn her away. "I don't want to talk right now," I say between tears.

Somehow I manage to wrestle down my back zipper and toss the beautiful dress in the corner, as if it's the dress's fault that my date never showed. My mascara is ruined, half of it running down my face. I yank out every hair pin, tossing them on my dresser, destroying the beautiful hair style pin by pin.

Despite my anger, my foolish heart is happy that nothing terrible happened to Brent. He's a bonehead for cancelling the date and I really wonder what the "something" is that came up. Did he just get cold feet?

After thinking about it for several minutes, I don't care what Brent's excuse is. He cancelled at the last minute, and I'm furious with him. My impulsive fifteen-year-old-self jumps to the conclusion that I mean nothing to him. I guess I was just the convenient girl next door to invite until someone better came along. Or maybe he decided at the last minute he didn't want to go to the dance at all.

What I thought was going to be a dream-come-true evening has turned into a nightmare.

When we bump into each other at school on Monday, I give him the cold shoulder, and he does the same to me. We both stubbornly ignore each other for the rest of the school year. He's my sworn enemy for life.

~*~

My throat is scratchy by the time I finish my side of the story. Brent retrieves a bottled water from the tiny fridge under his desk, comes over and sits beside me, then hands me the water. I sip on the cool beverage while Brent looks at me with sad eyes.

"I'm so sorry, Libby," he says. "I wish I could have seen the hairstyle and that dress," he adds.

"Me too. I wanted so much to see your reaction."

We gaze at each other for several beats, both lost in our own thoughts. "Can we start over? Pretend the prom debacle didn't happen?" Brent asks.

I nod. "I'd like that."

He smiles. "Hopefully our older selves will communicate better going forward. Let's promise to talk things out if we make the other person angry or disappointed."

A small grin tips my lips. "We'll probably make each other angry many, many times knowing our track record."

He chuckles, then leans over as if he's going to kiss me. I tingle in anticipation as time slows down.

When his computer dings we both jump.

"What was that?" I ask in a breathless voice.

He leans his forehead against mine and groans. "My meeting in five minutes."

Reality crashes in and I spring to my feet. What if his meeting attendees had arrived early and caught us kissing in his office?

"I've got a job to do!" I shout. Tacking a professional expression back on my face, I add, "I'll be at my desk if you need me."

131

I flee the room like my pencil skirt is on fire before Brent has a chance to say another word. Sinking down at my desk, I ponder what Brent meant by starting over. Does it mean he wants to date me for real? Or are we still fake dating to appease his dad? Am I still just a means to an end where Brent gets the baseball organization and I get another broken heart?

Confusion mars my brow. So much for vowing to communicate better.

Nineteen – Where Do We Go from Here?

Brent

I groan as Libby flees the room as if her deliciously curve-hugging skirt is on fire. This meeting with Dad, our chief financial officer Greg, and Amelia our director of marketing sure comes at an inconvenient time. Libby and I were finally making progress at putting our rocky history behind us.

But she's also my assistant. That was evident by the way she jumped to her feet proclaiming she had a job to do. I was going to kiss her and that would break every one of Libby's rules. We need to keep it professional while we're at the office.

Confusion lodges in my gut. Libby's an excellent assistant and I don't want to lose her. On the other hand, I'm attracted to her and want to date her. *For real*. But maybe we should continue down the fake dating path? Keep our messy emotions out of it since she's still working for me. Once Dad hands over the organization, Libby and I can explore a real relationship. After I'm in charge, it won't matter that my girlfriend works for me. No one will question the relationship.

~*~

Dad hangs around after the lengthy meeting. Amelia had some great ideas for drawing in new fans. Our fan base demographic indicates that males between fifty and ninety are our mainstay. Amelia wants to entice a younger generation, including more women, to attend our games. Her information was eye-opening, and we all agreed to her plan, which means spending a larger chunk of the budget on marketing. Thank goodness I already signed Sam Hudson, because the budget is stretched as tight as a violin string.

"Son, your mom and I really enjoyed getting to know Libby better at the charity auction. She's quite a gal." Dad says, giving me a broad smile.

Luckily my office door is shut; Libby can't overhear what we're talking about. "She's very special."

He leans forward, clasping his hands on his knees and frowns. "But do you think it's wise to date your assistant? Things get complicated and messy quickly when you mix business with pleasure."

I frown. Dad has identified the major flaw in my plan, whether I want to admit it or not. I certainly can't confess to him that the ground rules between Libby and me is that we're *fake dating*. Our emotions aren't involved in the equation—or at least weren't supposed to be. Dad needs to believe what Libby and I have is real.

My confusion over whether to continue fake dating from earlier eases. Keeping this thing between Libby and me as a fake relationship is the right thing to do. It buys us time to get to know each other better. We can have a real relationship once Dad turns over the reins.

"I've only gone out with her one time! We're taking it slow. Our relationship here at work is purely professional, I assure you." Heat floods my cheeks knowing that an hour ago I almost kissed my assistant right here in this office.

Dad stares at me as if he's trying to read my mind, then he shrugs. "Okay, I hope you two know what you're doing. It's not fair to Libby if you're dating her just to appease me, trying to fulfill my ultimatum."

Oh boy, Dad is astute! No wonder he led this organization from being a mid-market team to being one of the top teams in the country. Guilt sits in the pit of my stomach.

I shake my head vehemently. "After we started working together, I realized my attraction to her. If we hadn't had the prom debacle back in high school, I'd have been dating her before now."

Maybe even married her.

"I'll trust your judgement, son," Dad says as he stands. "Good luck keeping the line between personal and professional clear." His eyes bore into mine, his warning hanging between us.

Without another word, he turns and strolls out of the office. I hear Libby and him exchange friendly conversation. It's obvious both Mom and Dad like her.

I'm going to reiterate with Libby sticking to the rules, the ones she crafted. We can keep this relationship from becoming complicated as long as we follow the rules. Right?

Twenty – Between a Rock and a Hard Place

Libby

I decide that the only way Brent and I can keep a clear line between our professional and personal relationship is to make sure we follow the rules. We came close to being found in his office kissing! How embarrassing and unprofessional.

I'm totally caught between a rock and a hard place. I want to work for Brent: I need this job, and it's so much better than Harv's Diner. At the same time, I'm attracted to my boss. He's the boy next door, my brother's best friend, and my high school crush. We don't have to mention the decade we spent as enemies.

I wish we could roll back time and get a do-over. Since that's not possible, our do-over starts now, how we handle our relationship going forward. A line in the sand between business and pleasure should help alleviate any awkwardness. We can work together at the office, while also exploring our burgeoning relationship outside the office—a real relationship that has a future.

After Mr. Masterson leaves, I march back into Brent's office with the intent to reinstate the rules and discuss moving our dating forward from fake to real, juggling business and pleasure, with the goal of a genuine relationship. My heart zings with excitement.

"Libby, please sit down," Brent says, looking up at me with a smile.

I sit, returning his smile. Before I can launch into my prepared speech, Brent says, "Dad reminded me of how difficult it is to maintain a professional and personal relationship. How easily the lines become murky."

Nodding, I say, "I agree. We just blurred the lines, and the lines need to be clear."

Obviously we're on the same page! This is a relief.

"The rules you suggested are a good way to get us back on firm footing. We also need to remember that our relationship is fake. If, after Dad hands over the team to me, we want to pursue something real, we can. For now, we're fake dating. That will keep any messy emotions out of this."

Say what? We're still fake dating?

My heart plummets, realizing that in fact we are not on the same page. I'm not sure we're even in the same book.

I thought we were going down the path of reinstating the rules here at work but dating for real. Exploring a true relationship, with no ulterior motive to satisfy his dad. Yet all Brent seems to care about is taking control of the team.

He doesn't care about me.

It feels like a giant boulder just fell on me, squashing all my hopes. My lips wobble and I furiously blink back tears. "I'm glad you cleared that up. I'll email you the rules again so you can refresh yourself on them," I croak out over the lump in my throat.

Brent's brows draw together. "You understand why this will be easier, don't you? Fake dating gives us an opportunity to get to know each other, without any expectations for a future. Like dipping our toe in the pond, without getting our clothes wet." He grins as if he's just revealed the secret to a successful relationship.

You dummy! I want to yell at his handsome face. He's applied logic to something that defies logic—love. I'm already falling in love with him, but now that he's exposed his sincere feelings, there's really no hope for us. I'll shore up my acting skills and give the performance of my life so he can get what he wants—the team. He doesn't want me. It was never about "us" becoming real.

"Of course. This will be easier," I say before striding back to my desk. When I glance over my shoulder Brent looks confused, as if he finally picked up on the bad vibes emanating from my body.

Tonight, I'm going to start my internet job search again. I had stopped doing that for several weeks, especially since I enjoy working here. But there's no future for me here.

Professionally or personally.

Sitting back at my desk, I email Brent.

Boss, here's the rules. Please memorize them and follow them to a T –Libby

Twenty-One – You Got What You Asked For

Brent

Ever since Dad suggested that it would be awkward to have a professional and personal relationship with Libby, that's exactly what happened. After I gave the speech about following the rules and keeping our dating on an even keel, Libby is stiff, polite, and detached. She keeps our conversations at the office to a minimum, asking me to submit requests via email. She declines all invitations to eat lunch together. And she never brings me coffee anymore. Basically, I got what I asked for.

I want the fun Libby back!

The Libby who, last week, spent an entire lunch hour with me, eating deli sandwiches and discussing who was the weirdest teacher in high school. I made some good arguments for the biology teacher, Mr. Peabody, with his ugly sweaters with dog hair all over them. He always started class by citing the newest discoveries in flora and fauna as if teenagers would find the latest algae or microbe species enthralling.

But Libby made a strong case for the librarian, Miss Taylor, by enumerating all her quirks. Her massive purse that seemed to produce more stuff than Mary Poppins—an umbrella, a gooseneck reading lamp, a container of wet wipes that held a lifetime supply. Her half glasses that she'd scowl at you over. Her long flowy skirts worn with knee-high socks and combat boots.

I haven't laughed so much in years.

Then there was our heated lunchtime debate just a few days ago, this time while eating Asian wraps from a food truck named The Green Frog, about Han Solo's claim to have made the Kessel Run in less than 12 parsecs. Libby claimed that Han lied since a parsec isn't a measure of time, while I argued that Han took a shortcut. I still think I won that one since *Solo* basically confirms my stance. Of course, not all stalwart *Star Wars* fans accept the new movies as canon . . .

But that's another debate I was looking forward to having.

After long frustrating meetings with the executive team, Libby would bring me a cup of coffee from the break room, my favorite robusta blend with a splash of real cream from the fridge. She'd accompany it with a pastry if any were left. Whenever the meeting included Dad—who can be rather long-winded—she'd hide a Long John or apple fritter in her desk, ensuring I got one. The pastries are almost as sweet as she is.

I really, really want the fun Libby back!

Mom's ringtone plays, jolting me from stewing over the relationship with my assistant. I'm still at home dawdling over coffee and a bagel, trying to come up with a set of new rules that gives me the old Libby back.

"Hello?"

"Brent, dear! So glad I caught you. I'm calling to remind you about the Masterson family reunion picnic on Saturday."

I groan internally and pinch the bridge of my nose, an instant headache forming between my eyes. "Yes, Mom. How could I forget with your seven evites and sixteen email reminders?" She's inundated me with reminders for weeks now.

She cackles. "Well, you never know what works best."

"I'm coming," I say hoping the verbal commitment will stop the barrage or reminders.

"Please bring Libby too! She's delightful, and I'm sure the rest of the family wants to meet her."

Translation: Mom blabbed to Laverne, Shirley, and several of her cousins about my new girlfriend.

"Okay, I'll invite her."

"Oh, no need! I'll include her on the evite and email reminders."

"Thanks, Mom," I say in a snarky tone as she hangs up.

I text Libby, warning her about the invitation deluge that she's about to receive. Hopefully Libby continues to be a good actress. I need her to convince my family that we're dating for real.

I think that would have been easy with the old Libby. This fake dating and strictly adhering to the rules is becoming problematic. Wish I had just left things where they were before Dad offered his advice.

Twenty-Two – Breaking Another Rule

Brent

When I arrive at work, Libby's at her desk, staring at her laptop screen. She barely looks up as I pass by.

"Good morning, Libby! I'll be leaving around ten for the airport." I'm flying off with the team for their two games in San Francisco, then returning home on the Friday night redeye, knowing full well I've got to be home in time for the family picnic.

She grunts, eyes still focused on the screen.

"Did you get the invite from my mom for the family reunion on Saturday? I hope you can come." I try to enthuse my voice with excitement over the family shindig, but in reality I'd rather be stuck in an all-day meeting with Dad and the executive team.

Her eyes swivel to mine, a scowl tipping her lips. "Yes, I got three evites and six email reminders."

My lips twitch as I try to suppress a grin. I'm not sure whether Libby's grumpy look is due to the plethora of reminders from Mom or from my presence.

"I assume this is required attendance for me to qualify for the hazard pay?" Libby spits out.

My jaw drops; her question sounds so mercenary. She's still only agreeing to fake date me for the bonus? I didn't even have to twist her arm to go to the gala, so why is she bringing this up now? Dad's dumb suggestion comes back to haunt me once again. Why couldn't I just leave things as they were? *Sort of fake dating. Sort of real dating. That sort of thing.*

"Correct," I say in a grumpy voice, then stride off to lick my wounds and hide in my office.

~*~

"Charlie is here to pick you up," Libby says as she pops her head into my office. Her tone drips with professionalism and politeness. My molars grind together.

"Already?!" I lost track of time and still have a laundry list of work items I want to discuss with Libby before I leave.

She arches an eyebrow and gives me a "you're the one who can't keep track of time" glare, albeit in a detached, professional manner.

I pinch the bridge of my nose, trying to ward off the impending headache. "Can you ride with me to the airport? I need your help on several things."

She bites her lip and hesitates, then nods. "Sure. It'll give me a chance to catch up with Charlie about the new grandbaby."

Ouch! Nothing like sticking the knife in and twisting it.

I grab my overnight bag, slip my phone in my pants pocket and my laptop into its carrying case, and follow Libby to the elevator. She looks so put together in her neatly tucked blouse and wrinkle-free skirt, her hair pulled back into a tidy ponytail. I want to haul her into my arms and muss up that look a bit. *A lot.* Instead, the ride down to the ground floor is decidedly chilly. No fun banter or small talk or rumpling her buttoned-down look.

I slide into the limo first and Libby tumbles in after me. Her high heel catches on the door frame and she almost sprawls in my lap. I long to tug her in for a kiss, but I remind myself this is technically during work hours.

"Sorry!" she says in a breathless voice, righting herself and sliding to the far side of the seat. Before I reinforced the rules, we both would have laughed about her inelegant entry.

This monkey suit has been bothering me all morning. The shirt sleeves are too short and the collar too tight. I typically change in the office restroom into casual clothes for the flight, but I didn't have a chance. Shrugging out of my suit jacket, I hand it to Libby.

She folds it neatly and sets it on the seat between us. The tie comes next, then I start unbuttoning my shirt.

Libby's eyes go wide. "What are you doing?" she yelps, clutching my tie to her chest like I'm performing in a *Magic Mike* trailer.

"Getting out of this shirt," I say. Her startled expression tells me that I should probably just ride in the constricting shirt until we get to the airport. "I'll just change really quick," I add, desperately wanting to get into the T-shirt in my overnight duffle as soon as possible.

Once my shirt is unbuttoned, it hangs open, providing a peek at my bare chest. The chest she hasn't seen since high school—one time during an awkward encounter in gym class when I was still in my gangly stage. My face heats. *Maybe this wasn't such a good idea.*

Libby's wide-eye stare meets mine and she gulps. I want to tell her to turn around or close her eyes, but the way she's looking at me turns my knees to mush and renders me mute. The vibes of attraction zing between us like an electrical current. She's obviously not immune to me and all the weightlifting I've done since being the scrawny high schooler.

"Charlie, stop the car. I'll get out here," Libby rasps.

He does as she requests without saying a word. *Who's the boss here?* Libby hops out, still clutching my tie. Spinning around, she strides off down the sidewalk. I slide out of the limo after her and yell, "You've got my tie! I need that."

Turning on her heel, she strides back and flings the tie at my head. Pointing a finger in my face, she says, "I'm amending the rules. No removing your shirt in the office!"

"We're not in the office!" I yell at her retreating back. She ignores me, moving at an impressive clip in those high heels.

Passersby take a wide berth around me as I stand on the sidewalk, my shirt flapping open, gawking as Libby disappears into the crowd. Obviously some of them witnessed our fight. Red faced, I climb back into the limo, wondering what just happened. Glancing down, I confirm she'd see more of me in my swimming trunks than this. *Why the overreaction?*

I look out the back window, trying to get a glimpse of Libby. "Charlie, is this area safe? I'm worried about her walking back by herself."

"We've only driven two blocks, sir. This area isn't dangerous, and look at all the lunch crowd milling about," he says, his deep voice soothing my concerns.

He's right, there are people everywhere, heading off to the many eateries in the area. "Maybe we should turn around and pick her up?" I say, still feeling the aftershocks from our mini fight.

"You will be late to the airport if we do that," he reminds me.

I slouch back in the seat. "Okay, let's go," I say in a defeated voice. The old Libby would have giggled and hid her eyes when I tried to change my shirt. But I've messed up everything, and every interaction between us now is awkward, frustrating, and cringe-inducing.

"I think she's mad at me," I say, staring as the landscape changes from office buildings to bumper-to-bumper traffic.

A belly laugh roars out of Charlie's mouth. "Excellent read of body language, sir," he says as the limo crawls onto the busy freeway.

Twenty-Three – A New Rule and An Epiphany
Libby

When I get back to the office my anger has dissipated like a popped balloon. I know I overreacted to Brent unbuttoning his shirt. I could have closed my eyes or turned away, but when I got a glimpse of his well-developed chest, I panicked. He's no longer the scrawny guy from high school. *Wowza!*

How am I going to resist him after seeing that? He's sure filled out, confirming that Brent is now all man. The boy I had a crush on has grown up, making him even more potent to my senses.

Trying to maintain a professional detachment to him here in the office is becoming more and more difficult. Plus, now I've got to attend his family shindig on Saturday and pretend to be his girlfriend. All the while keeping my true feelings for him under lock and key. Our fake dating scheme was a mistake.

Big time.

I didn't intend to bring up the hazard pay when he asked me to attend the family reunion. That slipped out in a testy moment. I'd attend even without getting a dime. I've fallen that much in love with the bozo. My poor heart is going to be crushed when we break up.

Focusing back on work, I amend the rules to include the new clause about shirts—or any clothing item for that matter—and shoot Brent an email with the update. Turning back to my to do list, I tick off tasks, knowing Brent is going to send me fifty more as soon as he gets to the airport.

~*~

The next morning, I take Fred and Wilma to the dog park. For a guy who claimed he takes his dog to the park often, Brent's only been here a few times. Whenever he's on a trip, like he is now, I take care of Fred and walk him. Even when Brent is home, since I'm his assistant, I'm the one to mostly walk Fred. See the pattern?

Both dogs have the sweetest temperament. They were from a litter that had been abandoned along the highway. Although they are of unknown pedigree, the dog rescue thought they had some Dalmatian in their ancestry, since both are white with black spots. Wilma has the cutest spots on her face, like she's wearing a mask.

Fred is the more timid one of the pair. Wilma has never met a stranger, human or canine. As I watch the two of them playing, Wilma is always the one who instigates meeting another dog. I chuckle when I remember how she ran off the Great Dane that was twice her size.

It's a gorgeous day, blue skies without a cloud to be seen. A light breeze ruffles the leaves in a nearby grove of trees. The perfect weather makes me long for Brent to be here and enjoy this with me. *That darn man! He draws me in like metal to a magnet.*

I sit on one of the benches sipping a large mocha Frappuccino—my reward to myself for walking to and from the dog park. The 1.8 mile vigorous walk will easily burn all the calories I'm consuming with the high-fat, sugary drink. *Not.*

Content to sit here and watch the dogs play and the passersby pass by, I catch sight of a well-dressed lady and a large white Poodle approaching. My eyes widen when I recognize Mrs. Feldman. Wishing I had something to hide behind, I put my coffee cup up to my face and look down at my feet, hoping she doesn't recognize me.

"Libby!" *Not only does she recognize me, she remembers my name.* The woman walks briskly towards me after letting her dog off leash into the gated park. Wilma instantly comes over to the poodle while Fred hangs back. My dog and Mrs. Feldman's dog excitedly wag their tails, then start sniffing each other in embarrassing places, as dogs do. Thankfully people don't greet each other like that.

With nowhere to hide, I smile and say, "Mrs. Feldman, so nice to see you again."

She settles onto the bench beside me. A cloud of her overwhelming perfume tickles my nose and I sneeze.

"Bless you," she says, the movement of her head rousing more scent to float my way. Maybe it's hairspray instead of perfume. I stare at her beehive hairdo, suddenly mesmerized by how much she looks like Marge Simpson—without the blue of course.

"Elizabeth is just tickled pink that you and Brent are dating," she says without the usual conversation starters like commenting on the weather.

"Oh, is she?" I say, hoping that Brent's mom hasn't told everyone she knows, because this fake arrangement isn't going to end in a happily ever after like in the fairy tales.

Mrs. Feldman nods. "Elizabeth is so excited that she's already reserved two dates at the Wilshire Gardens in October. Just in case," she says with a wink.

Guilt lodges in my throat. Not only is our fake dating going to end up crushing me, but it's also going to end up hurting other innocent parties, like Brent's sweet mom. The epiphany hits me in the face like a slap. When we break up, more hearts are involved than just mine and possibly Brent's. Although, come to think about it, his heart will be just fine once he gets full control of the team.

Speechless after Mrs. Feldman drops that bombshell, I listen as she describes her latest exercise craze, weighted hula hoops. Apparently this atrocious-sounding exercise is a low-impact form of cardio that helps burn fat and builds core strength. None of those things sound the least bit appealing to me.

"It even improves flexibility and balance," Mrs. Feldman enthuses. "You simply must try it, Libby. I'll text you where and when my class meets," she adds.

I meekly nod, give her my cell number, and say, "It might be difficult to fit this into my busy schedule, what with dating Brent and all."

She grins. "He's welcome to attend as well!"

Wouldn't that be a sight? If thinking about Brent didn't rip my heart to shreds, I'd laugh at the thought.

Twenty-Four – Meet the Mastersons

Libby

Brent's trip keeps our paths from crossing at the office for the rest of the week, which is great. After the embarrassing shirt incident, I needed time to regroup. The break from the awkwardness is a relief.

Saturday dawns bright and sunny, another perfect California day, especially for a family reunion. My inbox has been flooded with reminders about the party from Brent's mom. Last evening Brent texted me that he'll pick me up at eleven, with the picnic scheduled to start around noon.

"Maggie, I need your help!" I yell after looking through my closet for a suitable outfit. She jogs in with Wilma close at her heels. Since Maggie usually works from home and I now work in the office, my puppy has become her constant shadow. If Fred were here, he'd be right beside Wilma, but I dropped him off last evening at Brent's apartment, making sure I didn't bump into his hunky owner.

"What do you need, amiga?" Maggie asks.

"I don't have anything to wear to Brent's family reunion."

Her eyes widen. "Oh my! You're meeting the relatives? That's a big step to go to a family function with him!" She holds up a hand for a high five, her grin spreading from ear to ear.

Sagging down on the end of my bed, I say in a flat voice, "It's another fake date."

"After that spectacular kiss at the charity auction he still wants to fake date?!" she yelps, flailing her hands about. My roomie is always so dramatic.

I couldn't bring myself to tell her about the recent developments. I've been doing my best not to think about them. "Yeah," I sigh. "He thinks that will keep our relationship on even footing, so we don't blur the lines between business and pleasure. With fake dating we won't get serious about each other."

She sits down beside me and gently puts her arm around me. "How's that working out?"

"Terrible! I'm constantly fighting my attraction to him. Our relationship has become one awkward encounter after another. We don't have fun together anymore." My voice sounds whiny, like a petulant child.

"That's not good. Should you contract a viral stomach bug and bow out of today's picnic?"

I wrinkle my nose. Leave it to Maggie to come up with a plan like *that*. "I probably should. But I promised Brent's mom that I'd come." Mrs. Feldman's words slap me in the face. Our fake dating ruse keeps growing and growing, and Brent's sweet mom is going to be so disappointed when we fake break up. *Or is it a real breakup even though it was fake dating?*

She slaps her knee and hoots. "Libby Griffin, you've fallen for the guy, haven't you?"

"Yep," I admit reluctantly, unable and unwilling to lie to Maggie and myself any longer. Looking straight at my friend, I say, "That's a big mistake, isn't it?"

Her expression becomes thoughtful. "Maybe not, if he's also falling for you. At some point he'll have to admit it!"

My spirits lift slightly. Could he be falling for me, and that's why our interactions are so awkward and uncomfortable? He knows he should keep things professional, but he's fighting his attraction, making him grumpy and cranky. The thought sends my head spinning. *Can I get him to fall for me for real?*

Maggie leaps to her feet. "I have just the thing for you to wear!" She runs off down the hall to her room, Wilma hot on her heels.

~*~

151

"Do you think a dress is okay for a picnic? What if they want to play sandlot volleyball?" I chew on my lower lip as I stare at my reflection in the full-length mirror. The dress is very flattering. The spaghetti straps leave my shoulders bare. The bodice hugs my figure in all the right places, the skirt flaring out at my waist and the hemline hitting me mid-thigh. Sky-blue is a great color with my brown hair and my complexion, and the strappy sandals make my legs look longer.

Maggie laughs. "Would you even consider playing volleyball?"

"Well no. But that's not the point!"

My roomie pats me on my back. "You'll still be able to participate in a raucous game of hearts."

I love playing cards, and this dress won't inhibit me from doing that. "Okay, I'm ready."

Ding! Dong!

My heart leaps in my chest and my palms instantly turn sweaty. Despite being annoyed at Mr. Bigshot, I'm still massively attracted to him.

I answer the door and my heart stops. Brent's wearing tight blue jeans and a polo shirt that hugs his chest (I still can't get the bare version out of my head), and his hair isn't in his usual perfectly groomed business style. He's let it go wild and free, and my fingers itch to run through the messy locks, putting them in some semblance of order. *On second thought, leave the hair alone, this rumpled look is very sexy on him.*

"Are you ready?" he says in a raspy voice after surveying me from head to toe. The uncertain look on his face makes me wonder if he's afraid that commenting on my appearance might break one of the rules. Thinking back, have I added 'no compliments about appearance' to one of the amendments?

He swallows, his Adam's apple bobs up and down. "You look beautiful, Libby," he says, then holds up a hand. "Please don't remind me which rule number I just broke."

A small grin tracks across my lips. "How about no rules today? Just you and me attending a fun family outing." The idea slips out of my mouth, echoing my real feelings. I'd love to attend the reunion without having to worry about rules and the fact that this date is fake.

One eyebrow arches. "That sounds great, but I'm not sure we can label this outing as fun."

I grin. "Nonsense, Mr. Masterson. Laverne and Shirley will provide all the entertainment we need."

He laughs as we walk to his car. My heart approves when I see that there's no Charlie and no limo today. Brent's driving me himself.

~*~

The reunion is at Brent's parents' house—correction, mansion—and the picnic is being held in the sprawling backyard. My eyes about fall out of my head when Brent leads me through a side gate that opens onto a meticulously landscaped acreage sporting a swimming pool, tennis courts, an outdoor kitchen, and enough patio space and chairs to host two baseball teams. I knew the organization was doing well, but I didn't know it was doing this well. The Mastersons have really improved their position in the world since moving away from Pecan Street.

The Masterson clan is massive; there's so many of them I lose track. Kids are splashing in the pool and women of all ages are bustling in and out of the house carrying dishes of food. Guys dressed casually like Brent are chatting over beers while steering clear of the food prep.

Brent sticks to my side during introductions—introducing me as his new girlfriend, but only for purposes of hoodwinking his father, I'm sure. The younger aged relatives don't drill Brent about "us." They mostly wave, while all "The Grands" do more than their fair share of interrogation. Brent's cute nickname for his great-aunts and -uncles and his grandmother sticks, and I like it.

"Aren't you the gal from Harv's Diner?" Laverne says, squinting through her bifocals at me.

"She is, but Libby now works for me," Brent says.

The older lady snorts. "So, which is it? She works for you or she's your girlfriend?"

I feel a bit like a third wheel as they discuss me in front of me.

Brent shifts back and forth on his feet. "Both?" His reply sounds uncertain and wishy-washy, so I leap into the conversation.

Grabbing his arm, I tug him closer. "Brent, sweetie, don't you want to tell her how we fell in love over the Xerox machine?" I assume the older set will relate better to this term than "multi-function copy and print center" which is just too much of a mouthful anyway.

I playfully bat my eyes at him, while he turns beet red. Embarrassing my grumpy boss in front of his family is going to be fun. He deserves it for coming up with this lamebrain fake dating scheme in the first place.

Laverne leans forward. "Yes, tell me all the juicy details!" she says directly to me, a huge smile lighting her face. "Did you get any toner on each other?" That doesn't sound the least bit romantic, but Brent's grandmother's drooling look hints that she's possibly had experience with something like this. *Did she have an office fling back in the day?*

"Oh, look! Mom's trying to get our attention," Brent says. "We'll talk later, Grandma," he adds, then propels me at lightspeed across the yard towards where his mom is putting out what looks like potato salad. *Yum! My favorite.*

He skids to a stop about halfway across the lush lawn and whispers, "What are you doing, Libby?"

"Meeting your family," I say, blinking up at him with an innocent expression.

"But we didn't agree to embellish the story!" he sputters.

"Do you already have a cover story in mind? Please share it with me, so I know all the details."

He groans. "Libby, can't we be vague? This is all fake, so why add any extraneous details?"

His comment is like throwing ice water on my fun. "Fine, I'll let you explain everything," I say between gritted teeth. My heart sinks. We've been here less than fifteen minutes and we're already fighting.

He squeezes my arm, an apologetic look on his too-handsome face. "Come on, we can still have fun, can't we? Let's act like the old Brent and Libby before we muddied everything with the rules. Okay?"

I nod, albeit grudgingly. "Okay."

~*~

I manage to remain tight-lipped about Brent and me, letting him field innumerable questions. It's almost more fun watching him squirm at the inquisition than me making up fake details.

Great-Aunt Abigail (his grandmother's younger sister) asks, "How did you two love birds meet?"

"Libby's family lived next door when Mom and Dad used to live on Pecan Street."

"And you're just starting to date now?" She turns to Brent and smacks him with her purse. "Are you an idiot?"

I suppress a giggle as Brent's neck turns red. "When she started working as my assistant, we finally realized we're attracted to each other," Brent says, putting his arm around my waist. It's a wise choice not to mention The Debacle that previously derailed our relationship for eight years. We'd be here all day if Brent went into details about that.

The older woman makes a *tsk tsk* sound. "Mixing business and pleasure is tricky. You two just need to tie the knot. When she's your wife, there won't be any office gossip," Abigail says with a wink.

The sip of Coke Brent just took spews out his mouth. He coughs furiously and I pat him on the back, smiling benignly at his discomfort. "We just began dating," Brent wheezes.

"Nonsense! You two are perfect for each other. I can't help it if you're too shy to pop the question," Abigail replies tartly.

Great Uncle Benjamin, who just wandered up to join the conversation, yells, "Eh? Who'd you say the boy's dating?"

Since I'm standing right here with Brent's arm around me, I giggle.

"This is Libby. My girlfriend," Brent replies, tightening his grip on my waist.

The octogenarian looks me over from head to toe. "How'd you two meet? She's mighty pretty, you better not let this one get away." With his round bald head, the man reminds me of an older version of Charlie Brown. Glancing over at Abigail, she kind of resembles a well-aged Lucy. How'd these two get together?

And so it goes. Brent's pack of hard-of-hearing relatives ask the "how'd you meet" question over and over. At the third re-telling, I want to pull Brent aside and come up with a more romantic story, but I keep my mouth clamped shut. Brent repeats the rather snooze-inducing explanation again and again—how our families were neighbors and how working together made us realize that we wanted to start a relationship. At least part of the lie is the truth. The most boring part, of course.

A few of the older ladies roll their eyes at the lack of romance in story and some of the men call Brent out about how slow he's making progress in the "courtship department," as one of the old codgers calls it. By the time Brent has repeated the tale six times, I feel like we should have had cards made describing "how Brent met Libby" so we could hand them out.

It's a huge relief when Brent's mom calls everyone over for lunch, although I almost get trampled in the stampede to the picnic tables. I'm impressed with how quickly the octogenarian set can move when there's food involved.

"Sorry about that," Brent mutters as we follow the pack at a decidedly slower pace. He's holding my hand, and tingles run up my arm. Even though I'm still annoyed that this is a fake date, my feelings towards Brent can't be denied.

"It was so much fun watching your explanation and their reactions. I agree with Uncle Benjamin, you are a little slow in the courtship department," I say with a wink.

His eyes widen, but he doesn't say another word as we fill our plates. Let him stew on that for a while.

~*~

After lunch, Brent and I get roped into a game of cornhole with Abigail and Benjamin. I figure we won't even need to break a sweat playing these two. My fancy dress and sandals will be fine.

By the second game, I realize that I vastly underestimated The Grands. They beat us soundly in the first game, and we're losing in the second. Neither Brent nor I like to lose, so we've got to step up our game.

"You need to extend your arm out after your toss. Follow through," I say to Brent after his corn bag misses the hole for the third time in a row.

He gives me a stink-eye at my unwelcome coaching. "You're a fine one to criticize. Your tosses aren't much better."

Glaring at him, I slip off my sandals, thinking that the heels aren't conducive to a good cornhole toss. I carefully line up my throw and let go. The bag hits the hole but bounces off.

"Dagnabbit!" I mutter under my breath.

Brent snorts. "Dagnabbit? That's the best you got?"

"Cheese and crackers!" I fire back.

We stare at each other, then double over in laughter.

Game on!

Even though we're losing to two people more than fifty years older than us, playing cornhole poorly suddenly becomes outrageously fun.

Brent's next one-handed toss hits the platform but slowly slides off and into the grass. "Gee willikers! What does it take to hit the hole?" he exclaims.

I giggle at his phony outrage. Great-Aunt Abigail's eyes narrow, and she looks at us as if we've lost our minds.

We continue, each one of our tosses getting worse than the last. It's more fun trying to see how badly we can miss the hole and "swear" about it than when we were trying to win.

I swing my arm in a wind-up circle like a slow pitch softball pitcher, then let the bag fly. It almost hits Great Uncle Benjamin in the face. Brent puts his arm around me and giggles in my ear.

"Oh snap!" I shout for the benefit of our competitors.

"Are you two playing or just flirting?" Uncle Benjamin says after one particularly bad shot by Brent that sails over the cornhole platform and almost lands in the pool. We had tumbled onto the grass together in a fit of laughter. We plaster serious expressions on our face as we scramble back to our feet.

"Sorry. Sorry. We're playing," Brent says, holding up a hand. He ruins the moment when he bursts into another howl of laughter, sounding like a deranged hyena.

Pulling in a deep breath, I count backwards from one hundred, hoping to get my merriment under control. The game is tied, so we need me to actually hit the hole this time. Our terrible play must be throwing The Grands off their honed cornhole game as they're missing the hole as frequently as Brent and me.

Biting my lip, I focus on making this toss count. Brent stands directly behind me, whispering encouragement in my ear. Unfortunately, his sandalwood fresh scent and his warm breath on my neck are both terribly distracting.

The bag leaves my hand, flying through the air, aimed squarely at the hole. All four competitors hold our breath. When the bag hits the platform, it slides straight towards the hole. As if applying brakes, the bag abruptly comes to rest an inch short. The Grands exchange fist pumps and high fives at their victory.

I look at Brent and wail, "Corn Nuts!"

He picks me up, spins me around, and plants a sloppy kiss on my lips. We're so caught up in the moment, we don't even mention breaking the rules.

"Libby Griffin, you come up with the best cornhole curse words," he says with a grin. "But 'Corn Nuts' is the winner!"

I pump my fist over my head, while Brent lifts me up and hollers like we've won the lottery. His unabashed spontaneity takes my breath away. Time screeches to a halt when I notice that the crowd has fallen silent, every eye turned on Brent and me. He puts me down, and we stand awkwardly side by side, both our faces red.

"Well, son, looks like you finally figured out how to romance your girl," Uncle Benjamin says with a smirk.

My heart flutters at Uncle Benjamin's statement. When Brent and I let our guard down and forget about those darn rules, we get along famously—just like a real boyfriend and girlfriend. I wasn't acting, and I don't think Brent was either.

The cornhole game breaks up, The Grands clearly the better players. After Benjamin's comment, the crowd returns to whatever they were doing, and I watch as money exchanges hands.

Belatedly I wonder whether the octogenarian crowd were all betting on the outcome of the cornhole game. "I wonder if we were the favorites in the betting pool."

"I think they were betting on our relationship," Brent murmurs with a touch of chagrin.

My eyes fly to his. "Really? They'd do that?"

He nods. "Yep. And next they'll be placing bets on when we're going to get engaged."

I wince, realizing that I innocently played right into Brent's hands. His dad will turn the baseball organization over to Brent without question now after that performance.

A pang hits me in the chest knowing it wasn't a performance by me—everything I said and did was real. Gazing intently at Brent, I try to read his mind, but his expression remains inscrutable. Were the last few minutes an Oscar-worthy performance by Brent or were they real?

~*~

On the drive home, I say, "That was really fun! Thanks for bringing me." The moment the words exit my mouth, I want to suck them back in. This wasn't a real date, so I shouldn't be sharing my feelings about it.

Brent gives me a side-eye glance, something between confusion and regret on his face. "I'm glad you enjoyed yourself."

We fall silent. As the sedan eats up the miles back to my apartment, we morph back into stilted and awkward Brent and Libby. The Brent and Libby who don't laugh, don't tease, don't hug, and certainly don't kiss. We didn't fight one time over which rules we were breaking during the picnic, but now the rulebook sits between us like an elephant.

By the time we get to my apartment, the air inside the vehicle is almost suffocating. Rather than play out some awkward scene at my front door, I jump out as soon as the car stops. "See you on Monday," I say, then hightail it into my apartment. After the car drives away, the red taillights disappearing into the night, I realize that my poor heart can't take any more fake dates with Brent. *Something's got to give.*

Twenty-Five – Bumping into an Old Friend

Brent

Fake dating was a terrible idea. Libby and I had such a great time at the family reunion, but on the drive home everything became awkward again. Was she just pretending the whole time? I'm not sure that my heart can withstand any more fake dating with Libby. How do I turn this situation around—date Libby for real?

I spend Sunday knocking around my condo, trying to get Libby out of my head. I take Fred on a walk but avoid the dog park in case Libby and Wilma are there. Finally, when the four walls start pressing in on me, I head over to Burt's Sporting Goods. I sponsor several Little League teams, and some of their uniforms and equipment are wearing out. It'll be a nice surprise for the kids to get new stuff.

While looking at the shiny new aluminum bats, I just so happen to bump into Libby's brother, Griff. The way things ended between him and me when he retired from the team left a bad taste in my mouth. It created an awkwardness that Griff and I never had as kids, other than the ill-advised prom date with Libby that we finally got over. Now my interactions with both Griffin siblings are painful and uncomfortable. *How did our close childhood relationships come to this?*

"Brent! How are you doing?" Griff says, his friendly tone helping keep the unease between us at bay.

"I'm doing well. The team is keeping me busy now that Dad has stepped back from day-to-day operations."

"Yeah, Libby mentioned that your dad isn't around much. Has he fully handed over the reins to the team to you?" Griff smirks, knowing how much of a control freak Dad is.

I laugh. "Nope. And I don't have a clue when he's going to."

"What are you looking for?" Griff nods his chin towards the overflowing shelves. If you can't find the baseball equipment you're looking for here, you can't find it. "Has the equipment manager delegated purchasing team equipment to you?"

We both laugh. "No, I sponsor several Little League teams, and I was checking out new uniforms and equipment for them." I recently started sponsoring Charlie's grandkids' team. He was tickled when I made the offer after Charlie mentioned the two oldest kids were taking up baseball. I mostly came here to get them outfitted, but I may as well update the other three teams as well.

"That's a great gesture, Brent," Griff says, the laugh lines beside his eyes crinkling when he smiles. I'm instantly envious of Griff. What must it be like to be so happy all the time? I'm sure his sweet fiancée has something to do with it.

I shrug, preferring to stay out of the limelight because I don't want any publicity about me sponsoring these kids. "And what is a retired professional baseball player doing here?"

Griff gives me a look of chagrin. "Well, I joined a city league team and am outfitting myself to play." He pauses for several beats. "I know the league is nothing like the Bigs, but it satisfies my itch to get back into playing baseball."

A pang of guilt hits my chest at the fact that I wasn't the best friend to Griff when he got injured. My job as Manager of Player Personnel put me in an awkward position. I suddenly want to explain myself and try to make amends. "Are you free for lunch? Wally's Burgers is just around the corner."

Griff's grin is wide and familiar. "You know my weakness for that place! Let's go."

~*~

We're early enough to beat the rush. A waitress seats us near the back. Griff requested the isolated booth on the off chance a fan would recognize him. I wonder how often that happens anymore.

"What are you having?" I ask.

Griff chuckles. "I've actually tried every burger on the menu, so if you need a suggestion, I'm the man to ask," he says, jokingly pointing to himself.

My eyes widen. "No kidding?"

He nods. "After my injury, I got in a black funk, as Ari calls it. I thought because my career might be over that my life was over." He pauses to take a swig of water.

The pang of guilt hits even harder. Griff hid his suffering well, although come to think about it, I never even reached out to see how he was doing. "I'm sorry I wasn't a better friend," I blurt out, the guilt sitting in my gut like a boulder. Maybe I should pass on ordering anything with how I'm feeling right now.

Griff waves his hand in a dismissive fashion. "I know you were in an uncomfortable position. Being Manager of Player Personnel and being friends with a guy on the roster who you might have to get rid of," he says with a shrug. "I understand why you avoided me."

His understanding of why I was conflicted makes me feel marginally better, but I still feel like I should have been a better friend.

"Back to the burger story. When I finally emerged from the funk, after an intervention by several people—Grams and Gramps being two of them," he pauses and we exchange grins when he mentions his grandparents, who would get along famously with Grandma Laverne. "I decided to be more adventuresome. Find joy in the simple things in life. One of those was trying every one of Wally's Burgers." He grins, reminding me so much of my best friend from sixth grade.

"What's your recommendation?" I ask with a laugh.

"The Ground Cow is to die for," Griff replies.

I scan the menu for his suggestion, and then do a double take. "That one has cream cheese and Fritos on it?" I say in a surprised voice.

A belly laugh escapes from Griff's lips. "Trust me, those give it just the right flavor and crunch," he replies in a teasing voice.

We place our orders, both of us getting the Ground Cow—although me a bit more reluctantly than Griff. Once the waitress has flitted off, I say, "Griff, I'm sorry that I wasn't a good friend when you needed friends the most. It was difficult for me to separate our personal relationship with our professional one." I take a sip of my Coke, my throat suddenly feeling dry as dust. "Dad told me to back off our friendship. He feared that once your injury was rehabbed, you wouldn't come back full strength and we'd have to send you to the minors."

Griff winces. No big leaguer wants to get sent to the minors for anything other than a quick rehab stint, out of fear of languishing there for the rest of their career.

"Do you remember Roy Benson from a few decades back?" I ask.

"Yeah . . . he was the second baseman who tore his labrum, right?"

I nod. "Very few people know this, but Roy and Dad were buddies. When Roy came back from the injury he wasn't the same player, but he didn't want to admit it. After seeing Roy play in Spring Training, Dad sent him down to the minors. Roy was livid that Dad made a business decision without regard for their friendship. Dad had to make the best decision for the team, and he did, but Roy never forgave him. Eventually Roy retired and faded away, but Dad has always carried that guilt around with him."

Griff sits back in his seat, staring at me over his Dr. Pepper. He takes a few sips, then says, "Brent, I've never held my decision to retire against you. My shoulder wasn't going to ever get back to one hundred percent. I've come to grips with the fact that I'll never play professionally again."

I sag back in my chair, relieved that the guilt I've been carrying around over Griff is finally over. His honesty has lifted a big burden from my shoulders. "Thanks for letting me know that."

"How would you like to come on Wednesday night and watch some amateur baseball players? I can get you a ticket," he says with a smirk.

"I'd like that. I'll ask Libby to clear my calendar," I say enthusiastically, meaning it.

Our burgers arrive and we eat in silence for several minutes.

"Hey, this Ground Cow is tasty," I say, holding up my half-eaten burger. Two globs of cream cheese drip onto my plate.

"Told you so," Griff replies, puffing out his chest and grinning.

After a few more bites of our burgers, his expression changes to a thoughtful one and he says, "What about you and Libby? How is it working out having her as your assistant? You two mixed like oil and water ever since The Debacle."

I hide a grimace. He must not realize his part in The Debacle, or he doesn't remember it. "She's a great assistant," I say, avoiding the fake dating topic. If Libby hasn't mentioned it to her brother, no way I'm going to.

He arches an eyebrow. "You know, I hate that I chewed you out for asking Libby to prom. That was just the immature kid in me talking. I had a feeling you two would end up together some day. Guess I was wrong about that," he says with a shrug. His backhanded green light to Libby and me dating clears up that issue, although this time I'm determined to not let anyone else influence my desire to date Libby. Not Dad. Not Griff. No one.

Once we're done eating, Griff gives me the time and place for the city league game. "I look forward to seeing what skills you amateurs have. Maybe I can recruit a few for the team," I tease.

Griff laughs. "Maybe you should see us play first."

On my drive home, I feel good about the interaction with Griff. He holds no grudge against me like Roy did with Dad. I'm optimistic we can become close friends again.

It hits me that Dad gave me the same advice about Griff as he did about Libby. Don't mix your professional life with your personal life. Is Dad's opinion about that topic biased because of what happened with Roy? After this conversation with Griff, I'm convinced that we could have maintained our friendship this last year or two. Dad was wrong.

Can I make both a professional and personal relationship with Libby work? Maybe it's time to disregard Dad's advice and do what my heart is begging me to do.

Twenty-Six – History Majors Please Apply

Libby

Confused and frustrated about Brent's and my relationship, I spend all of Sunday searching the job sites with a vengeance. It'll be best to just move on. I don't see a way to salvage our relationship. It's become quite clear to me that Brent wants the team, it was never about him wanting me. Even though I love working for him, our personal feelings keep getting in the way. Brent's dad was right, you can't mix business and pleasure.

Towards evening, my eyes land on a new posting. I read it twice, not believing what it says.

Art History Museum Assistant Curator

My eyes eagerly scan the posting, my heart beating faster with every sentence. The Gunderson Museum was founded in 2018. Its funding comes from a trust from the Dean and Molly Gunderson family. The Gundersons recently increased the amount of funding, and the museum is expanding their American history collection, thus requiring an additional curator. The position is full-time, with benefits. A degree in American history is required, preferably with a minor in art history.

I sag back in my chair, shaking with excitement. The posting reads as if it was written specifically for me. Where is The Gunderson Museum at?

Reading further, my excitement quickly dulls. The Gunderson Museum is located just outside Cambridge, Massachusetts. I had hoped to obtain a position within drivable distance of my family. Ari and Griff are getting married soon, and I want to be here to play with their kids once they start having them. Plus, Grams and Gramps are getting up in age and may need my assistance at some point.

Tapping my finger on my chin, I stew about the posting. Massachusetts is the center of so much American history; it would be exciting to live and work there. With Boston not far away, there would be plenty of restaurants, social activities, and universities where I could obtain my advanced degree.

On the other hand, Massachusetts has cold weather and snow. Neither of those are particularly appealing in light of the balmy California weather I'm used to.

The posting is only two days old, with a deadline for next week. I have a couple days to think about this and still apply. Snapping my laptop shut, I grab Wilma's leash for a trip to the dog park. Getting some fresh air and exercise hopefully will help with my decision whether to submit my application.

~*~

Monday morning arrives and I still haven't decided what to do about the job posting. I couldn't sleep as I tried to work out pros and cons in my head all night. Wish Grams were here to talk this through with, but she and Gramps are on a month-long cruise. Maggie—who still holds out hope for a romance between Brent and me—would just try to talk me out of applying, so I don't mention it to her.

Brent isn't at the office yet, so I open my laptop and get to work on my never-ending to-do list. The building is quiet. I enjoy this time of day because I can get a lot done without interruptions.

My boss flies in right before his nine o'clock meeting. I quirk an eyebrow at his frenzied state. "Is everything alright?" I ask.

He grunts. "Dusty Sherman put in a request for a trade last evening. Since the trade deadline is tomorrow, I've got to drop everything and handle this."

"Do you need me to reschedule your nine o'clock?" He's meeting with Amelia and his dad to look at the marketing numbers from the new campaign.

Brent pinches the bridge of his nose. "Please clear my calendar. Get a meeting with Sherman and his agent for noon at that new fancy restaurant on Ninety-Fifth. Let's see if I can wine and dine the pitcher into changing his mind."

Brent disappears into his office, and I scramble to reorganize Brent's day.

~*~

Today is brutal, what with reorganizing Brent's calendar and fielding all the complaints about the last-minute changes. I'm ready to throw in the towel before ten a.m.

Brent and I don't argue or fight, but I feel like his minion, doing all the dirty work tasks for him. The fancy restaurant was booked solid, so Brent agrees to moving the Sherman meeting to the office. I haggle with three high-end restaurants before I find one willing to do takeout at the last minute. Apparently Mr. Sherman is quite the gourmet aficionado, and Brent wants to make sure the guy is impressed with the food.

After securing the food order, I decide that Uber Eats or Grub Hub isn't going to cut it for delivery of the pricey meal—I want to make sure everything is perfect since the organization is spending an arm and a leg on the food. Thankfully Charlie is available, and he takes me to retrieve the meal. "I'll just be a minute," I say as I leap out, managing to land gracefully in these high heels. *Why don't I keep a pair of tennis shoes at the office?*

"I'll be right over there," Charlie says as he points to a parking lot across the street. "Wave at me when you need me to pull up."

I nod and hustle inside the busy trendy restaurant. They have tons of five-star reviews online and the California Gourmet blog called the food "to die for."

"May I help you?" a snotty-looking hostess says as she looks down her nose at me. *Is my blouse unbuttoned?* I look down to confirm everything is secure and tucked. My ears finally register a buzz surrounding me, and as I glance around, it looks like every table is full. Since we're just a few minutes past 11:30, the lunch crowd is out in full force.

"I'm Libby Griffin. I have the takeout order."

"Oh, right. You're *that* Libby Griffin."

My brow creases. I may have been a tad bit over assertive when begging them to provide a takeout order at this busy time of day. After two other places turned me down, I was desperate. I remember mentioning that my best friend is an online influencer or something like that. I just failed to add that she's a fashion influencer. *Oops.*

"Pull around back to the loading dock and we'll bring out the food," she adds in a flat voice.

I jog out front and motion for Charlie. The limo glides to the curb in a few seconds. "Where's the food?" he asks.

"We have to pull around back to the loading dock."

He grunts his disapproval but does as I request. Almost before the limo stops, I jump out. A very crabby burly man dressed in white with a white apron tied around his pot belly meets me at the dock. He has a pushcart sitting next to him, and the entrées are apparently in those fancy silver servers with burners underneath that you can keep food warm in. Four of them are situated on the cart along with a couple bags of the side items.

"You can borrow these chafing dishes until three, but no longer," he says in a put-out voice. "Chef only agreed to his fine cuisine as takeout as long as you keep the food at the perfect temperature," he says nodding at the silver servers.

With our guests arriving at noonish, I should have plenty of time to get the servers back. "Thank you! That will be fine."

Charlie and I manage to wrangle the heavy dishes into the limo's surprisingly roomy trunk. The food smells delicious, so I'm encouraged that it will taste just as delicious when Dusty Sherman arrives.

"Light those burners as soon as you arrive!" the grumpy man says, then disappears back inside.

"He's a friendly sort," Charlie mutters under his breath.

Thankfully we get back to the office only a few minutes later. I start to sweat, remembering burly guy's warning about keeping the food at the perfect temperature. I couldn't have completed the process of unloading and getting the heavy dishes upstairs without Charlie's help. Fortunately, the front desk security guard came up with a pushcart for my use.

"Thank you, Charlie!" I say as I give the older man a hug, then trot off to the elevator pushing the overloaded cart. For a gal who doesn't like exercise, I feel like I've run a marathon.

After taking a few calming breaths, I set up the meal in the conference room. The aromas coming from the chafing dishes drive me crazy, but I resist trying a few bites of the food. Carefully lighting the small burners, I smile that the food is being kept at the perfect temperature. Plopping down at my desk and exhaling a deep breath, I wait for our guests to arrive in a few minutes. *Whew! I really cut it close.*

When our guests don't arrive on time, I start to worry. Are they stuck in traffic? Will the food be fit to eat when they finally get here?

I get panicky when one o'clock rolls by. Peeking in his office, I check with Brent to see if our guests have contacted him about being late. He's busy on the phone and ignores me.

My worries about whether the food will be edible escalates at the 1:45 mark. All this effort and expense to serve gourmet food and it's sat in those chafing dishes for almost two hours. Burly guy would give me a tongue lashing for sure.

Dusty Sherman and his agent finally stroll in at two o'clock. I'm fit to be tied and wish I could give Mr. Sherman a piece of my mind, but I bite my tongue. My fingers are crossed that the meal is still delicious—or at least edible.

"We're here to see Brent," Dusty says, not even bothering to apologize for being late. He comes across as a pompous well-paid athlete that doesn't give a fig about anyone else.

Why does Brent want to keep him so badly?

"Please have a seat. Let me get Brent for you," I say, rushing off to Brent's closed door.

When I enter, my boss is on the phone. His hair is a mess, and his suit jacket is in a heap on the floor.

"Dusty Sherman and his agent are here," I say.

He nods and says something to the other party, ending the phone call. I feel the bad vibes pouring off Brent as he shrugs back into his jacket and emerges from his office. Despite his rumpled shirt and disheveled hair, he looks gorgeous. He hides his annoyance at their tardy arrival from Dusty and his agent, plastering a friendly smile on his face. "Gentlemen, let's go to the conference room, eat, and talk about this." Brent says waving his hand towards the hall.

"We already ate," Dusty says.

I literally want to kill the star athlete. If the guy wasn't vital to the team, I'd go over, bean him with Brent's blue preferences folder, and tell him how rude he is. *On the bright side, maybe it won't matter that the food is now over two hours old.*

Brent's smile slips, but he quickly recovers. "Well, how about a little afternoon snack. There's food in the conference room."

They disappear and I hear the door to the conference room click shut.

Trying to focus on other tasks, I keep glancing at the clock, hoping they get done so I can return the chafing dishes to the restaurant. The burly guy made it very clear that they need to be returned by three. He'll probably fine me if I don't get these back on time. My heart pounds in my chest.

Tick. Tick. Tick.

When 2:30 comes and goes, I start to sweat.

Tick. Tick. Tick.

Finally at 2:45 the meeting breaks up. Sherman and his agent leave, and Brent immediately ensconces himself back in his office. By the look on Brent's face, I'd guess that the meeting didn't go well.

I call Charlie to come get me, then run into the conference room to load up the chafing dishes on the pushcart so I can bustle them down to the limo and back to the restaurant. Lifting each lid, my frown turns into an ugly scowl.

The food is untouched. I stomp my foot in anger and suppress a loud howl. If they weren't going to eat the food, we could have fed our staff. Now I've got to pitch the food out, something that irks me even further. If I had more time, I'd try to find somewhere we could donate the food to.

I reluctantly toss the contents of each chafing dish into black plastic bags. The lobster ravioli, spicy tuna onigiri, chicken Kiev, and smoked prime rib plop in a congealed mess into bags I fasten tightly for the janitor to discard. The food doesn't look overly enticing at this point. *Guess it was best that no one tasted the pricey meals.*

Wheeling the pushcart into the elevator, I take calming breaths.

Charlie helps me load the dishes again. He doesn't comment on the fact that we're going to be at least fifteen minutes late returning these. The man is a saint as he helps me, then drives as fast as traffic allows.

"I'd love to kill Dusty Sherman right now," I huff as Charlie drives. The frustration I'm feeling comes out in a long rant as I ramble on about the food fiasco, ending with, "And they didn't even touch it!"

"Miss Libby, don't let that Dusty guy get under your skin. He treats everyone with disdain," Charlie replies.

Why does Brent want to keep such a snotty kid so badly? Is being able to hurl a baseball over one hundred miles per hour more important than manners?

I run into the restaurant and approach the hostess stand. "I'm here to return your chafing dishes," I say in a breathless voice.

The hostess eyes me with the same insolence as she did before. "Go around back to the loading dock and I'll have someone meet you there," she repeats as if I'm a two-year-old.

The same grumpy guy meets us at the dock. "You're late with these. I should charge you another hundred bucks," he grouses. He crosses his beefy arms over his chest and scowls at me. His annoyed stance says that he's not going to be any help in unloading.

Charlie and I exchange looks but don't say a word. We unload the dishes where the guy requests, then get in the limo and pull away.

"Sorry he was such a rude person. What did they need those dishes for at this time of day anyway?" Charlie comments on the drive back to the office.

"I think he just wanted to make me feel bad," I reply as my lips wobble.

Charlie snorts. "You didn't deserve that, Miss Libby. You went way out of your way to get those dishes back."

For the first time all day, I feel appreciated. A tear leaks out of my eye and trickles down my cheek. By the time we get back to the office, I'm ready to apply for the Gunderson Museum job.

Twenty-Seven – Handing Over the Team

Brent

The trade of Dusty Sherman frees up budget to bring up a promising rookie from the minors. When I look back, trading Dusty was a blessing in disguise. Last week, though, I was fit to be tied. I was willing to live with his rudeness and haughty attitude, even when he showed up two hours late to the fancy lunch.

I know Libby did everything she could to bring in a last-minute gourmet lunch, but I was too annoyed at the time to thank her for her efforts. Instead, I shut myself in my office and didn't speak to anyone the remainder of the day. The next day I traveled with the team to an away game, so there's been no time to apologize to my assistant. I'll pad her hazard pay, trying to make up for letting my grumpiness freeze her out.

Libby ignored me when I came in this morning. With Dad arriving in ten minutes, I don't have time to try to make things right between me and my assistant. I'll sit her down this afternoon, explain my actions, tell her I want to date her for real, and hopefully get her to forgive me. We can put this fake dating scheme behind us, once and for all.

I hear Dad and Libby chatting about five minutes later. She laughs at something he says, then Dad strolls into the office.

"Dad, good to see you. Sit down," I say.

He looks relaxed in his bright lime green golf shirt and khaki pants. Knowing how much Dad would beat himself up when a player requested a trade, Year-Ago Dad would still be fretting over not signing Dusty Sherman. But my father appears laidback, as if he doesn't have a worry in the world. I guess mentally he's already handed the team over to me. While I'm happy that the pressure of this job isn't adding any more wrinkles to Dad's face, I worry that it's going to age me ten years in the next few months.

"Your mom and I found a home in Phoenix. We close on it by end of the month," Dad says as soon as he settles into his seat.

My eyes widen. "Really? That was fast. Are you going to be flying back and forth between Phoenix and California for a while?"

Dad chuckles. "No, the plan is to move to Phoenix."

I slump back in my chair, wondering what this really means.

"Brent, Mom and I are so pleased that you found a real girlfriend. Libby is everything we'd want in a daughter-in-law. You two looked so happy at the family reunion picnic that Mom and I decided it was time to give you full control of the team. Your relationship with Libby is on solid ground." He chuckles. "Mom's secretly hoping for a wedding in October, but you two should take your time."

Knowing that my relationship with Libby is rocky at best, I feel like a fraud leading Dad on by keeping my mouth shut. It doesn't feel remotely like Libby and I are headed to the altar in October— or any time.

I should feel elated, but I don't. This is what I wanted, for Dad to fully hand over the reins of the organization to me. I hired Libby and convinced her to our fake dating scheme to meet the terms of Dad's ultimatum. But I feel hollow inside knowing that this will put a quick end to the best relationship of my life. I'll take control of the team and lose Libby in the process. If I tell her now that I want to date her for real, she'll think it's only because Dad gave me the team.

Can I convince her to stay?

"Son, you don't look excited at this news."

I plaster a fake smile on my face. "I wasn't expecting this so soon, but I'm elated!"

We stand and shake hands. Dad slaps me on the back a couple times, grinning from ear-to-ear. "I couldn't leave the organization in better hands. But my golf game starts in an hour, so I need to get to the course. Let's sit down with the executive team tomorrow and make the announcement."

After he leaves, my rubbery legs won't hold me any longer and I flop down into the desk chair, trying to figure out how to keep Libby. How to convince her that our fake dating hasn't been so fake. At least for me. I feel like a big phony, wanting to have my cake and eat it too.

Once my emotions are back under control, I go in search of Libby, who's nowhere to be found. I want to get this apology and announcement off my chest as soon as possible and try to get our relationship heading in the right direction. No more fake dating.

Missy Gilbert strolls in and flops down at Libby's desk. What's she doing here?

"Do you need anything, Brent?" she asks while popping her gum. She's wearing black from head to toe along with black combat boots. But her hair is in pigtails, which kind of ruins the fierce aura I think she's going for.

"I'm looking for Libby?"

She shrugs, titling the chair back and planting her boots on the desktop. "Doris asked Libby to make an emergency run to get toner for the big boy printer. Marketing has a printing deadline today and there's no supply."

My heart sinks. "Okay, thanks," I mutter through gritted teeth, striding back into my office.

Hopefully I can catch Libby before the executive meeting tomorrow morning and set everything straight.

Twenty-Eight – Landing the Dream Job

Libby

I learn the next day that Brent is fully in charge of the team. His dad handed over the reins and his parents are moving to Phoenix. Our Oscar-worthy performance at the family reunion must have sealed the deal. *He didn't even care about me enough to tell me before the executive-team meeting.*

After the early morning meeting has dispersed, Brent calls me into his office. My feet feel like I'm wearing lead shoes as I walk in and sit down. He gives me a tentative smile.

"You got exactly what you wanted. Congratulations," I say in a forced voice.

Concern flits across his face. "Libby, I'm sorry I didn't have an opportunity to speak to you yesterday and tell you about this announcement."

His statement sounds a bit like a criticism, so my hackles rise. "Toner for that big brute of a printer is difficult to find," I say in a cranky tone. "I had to go to four office supply stores before I found any." Everyone hates that printer, but we're locked into a multi-year contract with it.

He bites his lip and looks like he wants to say something, then announces, "I want you to stay on as my assistant. We can even test out dating for real if you're agreeable."

Does he realize how clinical that sounds? What woman would accept that lukewarm offer?

My spine stiffens. "I'll stay on for a while, but Brent, be honest, do you really think a relationship between us would work out?"

His neck turns red. "Didn't you have fun at the family reunion?" he grumbles.

"I did, but wasn't that just for show?"

Shifting in his seat, he says, "Not all the time. I really like spending time with you."

Chewing on my lower lip, my eyes bore into his, trying to read his mind. I'd resign right now if I knew the outcome of my job application to the Gunderson Museum, but I don't. Unfortunately, I've got to keep this job until I land another one.

Needing to leave his magnetic pull before I crumble and agree to the crumbs he's willing to toss me, I stand and say, "Let's get through the transition of you to CEO before we attempt any dating."

He frowns. "That's fair, I guess." His voice is tinged with disappointment.

Does he not realize how lackluster his offer sounded?

We stare at each other for a few more uncomfortable beats. I'm hoping he will convince me why he wants to date me, express that he has real feelings for me. A little emotional begging or pleading would help, but he remains mute.

I wander back to my desk with a heavy heart.

~*~

Brent and I treat each other in a formal, stiff way for the rest of the week. If things were awkward when we were fake dating, this is worse. He's polite and respectful, but there's no appearance of the fun Brent anymore.

Even when we were trying to adhere to the rules, he'd forget and tease me every now and then. I enjoyed our heated lunchtime debates over the most trivial of topics—like who was the weirdest teacher in high school. I thought my arguments for Miss Taylor beat his for Mr. Peabody hands down.

A few days later I hear back about my application to the Gunderson Museum. I've been checking my personal email every evening, but when I spot an email in my inbox from

Curator@GundersonMuseum.com I'm afraid to read it, equally scared that it's a rejection letter or an invitation for an interview.

My palms sweat and I count to ten, then take three calming breaths. These are just delay tactics and I know it. Maybe Brent and I could eventually learn to work together in a more cordial and friendly environment, so my heart is holding out hope that I don't have to move on. But my brain knows the truth.

With one eye closed, I open the email and quickly scan it.

They want to interview me!

A grin splits my face. My fingers fly across the keyboard, scheduling a time for a Zoom interview later this week. Once I hit send, I'm committed. It's time to move on.

~*~

I'm so busy the remainder of the week helping Brent with the transition that I don't get nervous or anxious about the Gunderson Museum interview. Friday afternoon comes before I notice. I rush home over my lunch hour to do the interview.

Maggie gives me a thumbs up as I run into my bedroom and close the door. I made sure that my appearance today is one of a consummate professional with a neatly pressed blouse and black pants. Brent came in wearing blue jeans and a T-shirt, but he didn't even tease me about forgetting it's casual Friday. That's how much our relationship has deteriorated.

The head curator I would work for, Mrs. Zink, appears on the screen precisely on time. She looks to be in her forties, wearing a bulky sweater and wire-rimmed glasses. She smiles and waves, and I warm to her immediately.

"Hello, Libby! It's a pleasure to meet you," she says.

"Same to you! I'm so honored and excited to get to talk to you about this position."

We talk for the full forty-five minutes. She asks me probing questions about my degree, work experiences (I omit Harv's Diner), and skills, but she doesn't make me feel nervous, and I'm able to answer every question with confidence. I get a warm feeling that she would be a terrific boss. Before the Zoom call ends, she says, "Libby, I'd like to offer you the position. How about you fly out to Cambridge, we meet in person, and see if you like the place?"

I almost fall out of my chair. "Really?" I squeak. After collecting myself, I add, "I'd love that. When would you like me to come?"

She chuckles. "Would next Friday be too soon? You can spend the weekend here if that works with your schedule."

I agree and hang up. Fist pumping the air I shriek loudly, "I'm going to Cambridge!"

Maggie runs in, yanking me into a tight hug. "Oh my gosh, Libby! That's great news, but I'm going to miss you."

We hug as tears flow down both our cheeks. Mine are a mixture of happy and sad tears.

How weird is that?

When I return to work, Brent's gone for the day. He left a yellow sticky on my desk explaining that a sports agent asked him to play a round of golf to discuss a star hitter and a potential trade, so he won't be back for the rest of the day. Hopefully I won't have to scramble around next week bringing in a gourmet meal for the All-Star.

I sink into my office chair, disappointed that I now have to stew all weekend about asking Brent for next Friday off, especially when he's burning the midnight oil handling all the transition stuff. A twinge of guilt hits.

On Monday I march into Brent's office before I lose my nerve and inform him that I need to take a vacation day on Friday. He scowls at me for several long beats, but then nods.

"Have fun on your vacation," he says a bit grudgingly. I can't help it if he's working 24/7 during this transition. The suggestion that he ease back a bit almost slips out, but I stop it in time. His eyes drill into mine, as he obviously wants to know the details, but he recognizes the firm line between boss and employee that we've established over the last few weeks and doesn't ask.

Things remain professional and stiff between us all week, making me feel justified and confident that I'm making the right decision to move on.

I fly into Boston early on Friday morning and spend a delightful weekend looking at the area through the eyes of someone considering relocation. Mrs. Zink has a bevy of suggestions about places to visit, places to eat, and safe neighborhoods to live in.

When I drive down a street lined with vintage brick rowhouses in one of the recommended areas, I fall in love. There's so much history around me. Why didn't I try to find a job here sooner? It would have saved me a broken heart, that's for sure.

Cambridge is everything I imagined it would be and much more. Mrs. Zink and I hit it off even better in person than we did via Zoom. She's friendly, quirky, and very knowledgeable. It will be a pleasure working for and learning from her.

I eagerly accept the job and fly back to California, ready to give Brent my two weeks' notice on Monday.

~*~

With a nervous stomach (I couldn't eat a bite of breakfast) and heavy heart, I walk into the office on Monday. Brent's already here. He's been burning the candle at both ends ever since he took over from his dad. I'm worried about his health, but it's not my place to say anything.

Wanting to get this over right away, I poke my head into Brent's office. His rumpled appearance makes my heart lurch. He's got circles under his eyes and I swear I see a few new gray hairs in his messy mop. I want to go over, put my arms around him, and ask him how I can shoulder more of the load. Instead, I knock on the door frame. "Do you have a minute to talk?"

He rubs his eyes, then nods. "Please sit."

I take the chair across from his desk and drink him in. He's my dream guy, but it doesn't seem like I'm his dream girl. His haggard appearance screams that he's tired and worn out, after only a short time as owner. What's he going to look like in one year? Two years? Five years? Concern for him overrides what I've come here to do. "How long have you been here? You look terrible," I say.

He grimaces. "Well, gee, thanks," he says, a smidgeon of teasing in his tone. When I don't act like I picked up on the teasing, he huffs out a loud breath. "I never went home last night," he admits.

"What? Brent, you don't need to kill yourself trying to do this job," I say, genuine concern in my voice.

He shrugs. "Was there a reason you came in here other than to comment on my health?"

I wiggle in my seat; my leg jiggles up and down nervously. There's no gentle way to get this over with, so I rip off the Band-aid. "Brent, I'm giving my two weeks' notice. I've accepted a position as assistant curator at the Gunderson Museum."

He looks like he's just been slapped, and the shocked look on his face almost does me in. He runs his fingers through his already messy locks, then clears his throat. "Congratulations. I know you've wanted to land a position that uses your degree for quite some time."

His magnanimous acceptance of my announcement throws me off. I wasn't expecting this. "Thank you," I reply quietly.

"May I ask, where is the Gunderson Museum, I've never heard of it."

"In Cambridge, Massachusetts."

His expression changes rapidly before my eyes. He looks like someone who's been stabbed in the chest, but he quickly puts a neutral expression on his face. "Oh, I see. Wow, that's clear across the country."

"Yeah, that's one downside, especially since they have snow and cold temperatures," I say in a pretend teasing voice. When Brent doesn't even crack a smile, I plow on. "Griff assures me that he and Ari will help out Grams and Gramps if they need it."

Brent nods. "Can you put together a job posting, and we'll start interviews as soon as possible?"

With my heart cracking in two, I choke out a reply. "Sure. I'll do that right away." I guess my foolish heart was hoping that he'd try to convince me to stay. But we're truly done.

Twenty-Nine – I'm an Idiot!

Brent

After Libby walks out of my office, I sit here, hurting worse than if I'd been stabbed in the chest. I wanted to plead and beg her to stay, but at the same time I don't want to stand in the way of her advancing her career. Libby deserves to find her dream job.

I don't feel any excitement or joy in taking over the team. At one point, I thought this was all I wanted. Now, I feel like the one person who can make me happy is leaving me. *Why did I ever suggest the fake dating scheme?* Maybe if I'd dated Libby for real from the onset, I wouldn't be in this mess. Our relationship would be far enough down the road that the October wedding Mom is wishing for would be a real possibility.

I've lost Libby and I'm never getting her back.

~*~

Unfortunately, Libby's last two weeks fly by and I'm too scared to tell her how I really feel. Today is her last day. The staff had a nice sendoff party for her along with cake. I gave her a new laptop, and she nearly cried after she opened the package. Her old computer was so beat up I don't know why I didn't give her a new one sooner.

"Brent, I'm getting ready to leave," she says, hovering at my door.

I'd like to stall her departure, but that doesn't help my wounded heart.

"Well, good luck. You've been the best assistant anyone could ask for," I say, pulling her into a quick hug, then step back.

She looks up at me with tear-filled eyes and she blinks furiously trying to hold them back. I want to kiss her so badly and beg for her to stay.

"Can you give me a reason to stick around?" she asks.

The question takes me by surprise. I want to shout, *Yes! I'm in love with you. Please stay.* But I want her to have her dream job. It shouldn't be me who holds her back. "Libby, you got your dream job. You'll never have that here."

A tear slips out and slides down her cheek. My hand raises to wipe it off, but I drop it back at my side. If I touch her, I won't be able to let her go.

"Thank you for the job. I really enjoyed it," Libby says, strides out to her desk and collects the box her stuff is in, then she's gone.

I berate myself for being an idiot, but I'm not willing to do anything about it.

~*~

The new assistant is doing fine, but she's not Libby. She's been here solo for a week after shadowing Libby last week, and she's still learning the ropes. I don't remember a time when Libby was learning the ropes, she just knew what to do and did it well. But I'm kidding myself if I think that I'm missing Libby solely as my assistant.

I'm missing Libby. Period.

Her smile. The way she lights up a room and makes my heart flip. Her ability to keep me on my toes and challenge me at every turn.

I'm sitting at my desk nursing my broken heart when a commotion rises outside my office. It sounds like my new assistant is in a heated debate with a woman with a strong Spanish accent. I peek out my office door and Libby's roommate turns to me.

"You are an idiot, Brent Masterson," she says loudly, pointing a finger at my face.

An embarrassed flush heats my cheeks. "Let's talk in my office," I say after heads peek out of their office doors to watch me get a tongue lashing from Libby's extremely vocal roommate.

I quickly escort her into my office. The full head of steam she had outside my office carries right in with her. Pacing back and forth in front of my desk, she gestures wildly and yells at me in Spanish for several minutes. I don't understand a word, but her body language speaks volumes.

Eventually she sags down in one of my guest chairs with a scowl on her face.

"Are you done?" I ask.

She nods.

"Would you like to repeat any of that in English?"

A small grin twitches her lips. "You are an idiot for letting Libby go," she says in a slightly calmer voice.

"I didn't want to stand in the way of her dream job," I reply in a heated tone.

She stares intently at me. "I debated on whether to come here, but Libby begged me to drop something off. I should have just mailed it," she mutters.

What is she supposed to drop off? A nasty letter? A photo of the two of us ripped in half? A lump of coal?

"Do you love her?" Maggie asks, cutting off my wayward thoughts.

Fidgeting in my chair, I debate whether to tell the truth or lie. Under the woman's intent glare, telling the truth wins. "Yes, I love her," I sputter.

"Then why didn't you tell her that?"

I sigh. "I wasn't sure whether she felt the same way."

"You chicken! Of course she felt the same way."

Rolling Libby and my relationship over in my mind, I try to determine if she ever said she loved me or at least gave some very strong hints. "But she only agreed to fake dating when I agreed to hazard pay."

Maggie groans, digs around in her purse, and thrusts a paper at me. "Here, maybe this will convince you. Libby insisted that I drop this off."

She hands me a check, from Libby, made out to the baseball organization in the amount of her hazardous duty pay. I stare at it, dumbfounded. "But I don't understand," I say.

"Brent, she didn't want that money. She dated you for real. But she thought all you wanted was the organization, not her."

After retelling the prom debacle, we both agreed to communicate better going forward. *We sure failed at that, didn't we?*

I surge to my feet and start pacing beside my desk, needing to let off steam. "I want her!" I yell.

Maggie smiles at my distress. "So, what are you going to do about it?"

"Has she moved yet?" I ask in a panicked voice.

"As luck will have it, today is her last day here. The family is having a goodbye party for her tonight."

"Who's in charge of the party?" I ask.

"Grams. Do you have her phone number?"

A relieved laugh escapes my lips. "No, but I'm sure you will give it to me."

Maggie grins.

After she departs, I scramble to put in motion what I should have done two weeks ago if I hadn't been such an idiot. I've got several phone calls to make.

Thirty – The Blue Dress

Libby

"Libby, look what I found!" Grams says as she strolls into my bedroom, which is a mess because I'm still packing. She looks so refreshed and carefree after the cruise. She and Gramps returned a few days ago, both surprised and elated when I told them my job news.

"I didn't know you were stopping by," I say, confusion on my face.

"Maggie may have mentioned that you need a fancy dress to wear tonight."

I smirk. My roomie and best friend is such a meddler. She can't keep her nose out of anything.

"Seeing that you got reservations at the top of the Columbia Tower, yes, I need a fancy dress. The only one I have is the one I wore to the charity auction with Brent." At the mention of his name, my voice cracks and I frown.

"Well, you won't have to wear that one. Try this one on," Grams says, holding out the plastic-wrapped dress to me.

I pull back the wrapper and gasp. The blue dress looks as beautiful as it did when Grams bought it for me.

"It's the prom dress," I say in awe. "Do you think it will fit?"

Grams chuckles. "Well, you won't know until you try it on."

Grinning, I run into the bathroom, strip off my current outfit, and wiggle into the dress.

"It's a bit tight around the hips," I say in a dejected voice as I waddle back into my bedroom.

"I've got scissors, a needle, and thread! We can fix it!" Maggie yells from her room.

Grams and I both laugh.

~*~

191

Griff calls me as I'm getting ready for the fancy dinner.

"Hey, what's up?" I say as I answer.

He clears his throat. "Libby, are you sure you don't want to stay and try to work something out with Brent?"

My jaw drops. *Where is this coming from?* "Nope," I manage to croak out around my surprise. "We don't have a future together."

There's a tangible pause, the Griff says, "I'm the one who cratered your prom date with Brent. I told him my sister was off limits."

Even though I already know this, I exclaim, "Sebastian Griffin, stay out of my love life!"

My brother groans. "We've always been honest with each other. Are you absolutely sure you have no feelings for Brent."

My lips wobble. "Of course I have feelings for him," I whisper over the lump in my throat. "But it's too late for us."

"That's all I wanted to know!" he says and quickly hangs up.

What was that all about?

~*~

This is my first time dining at the top of the Columbia Tower. This restaurant is as glitzy and fancy as I thought it would be.

Wish Brent had brought me here.

Shoving that unwelcome thought aside, I stare at the faces of the people I love. Grams, Gramps, Griff, Ari, and Maggie all came here tonight to celebrate my new job and to wish me luck. My heart is filled with love, although there's still a broken piece because someone's missing.

Quit thinking about Brent!

A waiter wearing a black tux greets us and reads the daily specials. Between that list and the menu, there's so many yummy options.

"May I take your drink orders first?" he says.

The never-shy Maggie says, "I'd like a skinny margarita, meaning I want tequila on the rocks, with two lime wedges, and one orange wedge. Make sure you don't use even a drop of agave syrup. Are you with me?"

"Yes, ma'am," the waiter replies.

"I'll have a Budweiser," Gramps says.

"Make that a Bud Light, he's watching his weight," Grams adds.

"I'm not watching my weight!" Gramps replies, glaring at Grams.

The young waiter tugs at his collar as if it's suddenly too tight. He stares between Grams and Gramps with confusion on his face. It's going to be interesting to see what kind of beer Gramps gets.

"Do you have sweetened iced tea?" Grams asks, moving on from the beer debate. "I don't like the aftertaste of those artificial sweeteners. And they make me belch."

The waiter's eyes go wide at that confession. He glances at a couple staring at their menus three tables away. He's probably wishing he was waiting on them. I bet they wouldn't have disagreements over beer, and they certainly wouldn't mention belching. I do a mental shrug. While Grams and Gramps can often be embarrassing, I love them from the top of their gray heads to their toes.

"Well, young man?" Grams says sharply, reminding him of the question.

He clears his throat. "We sweeten our tea with real sugar, nothing fake."

"I'll take that," Grams adds.

Griff, Ari, and I all order ice water. I guess we're the boring ones in the bunch.

"I'll get these drinks ordered and then return to get your entrée selections," he says with a slight bow, then flees from the room.

"Whew! This place is high-end all the way," Maggie comments, ignoring the previously awkward few minutes.

"I planned an event here one time. Their food is delicious," Ari adds.

Griff laughs. "Where haven't you planned an event at?"

"McDonalds?" Ari says, then shakes her head. "No, I had a pirate-themed birthday party for a six-year-old there one time."

The table laughs.

Our waiter emerges from the back carrying a full tray of drinks. He's got it balanced rather precariously, but he manages to get to our table without incident. He quietly and efficiently distributes the beverages. Gramps gets a full-strength Budweiser, but I notice the waiter discreetly turns the label away from Grams.

The A+ server sets his tray on a nearby holder and takes our entrée orders. We manage to get through the process without any disagreements or embarrassing comments.

Once the waiter leaves, Griff raises his glass and offers up a toast. "To the best sister in the world. Good luck in your new job, but we all wish it wasn't so far away!"

The table seconds his sentiment, almost making me second-guess my decision. *Almost.*

"Libby, you're going to be the best assistant curator on the east coast. I'm so proud of you," Grams says.

"How do you know? There's a lot of them," Gramps says while Grams elbows him soundly.

"You old coot, this is a toast. You're supposed to say nice things," Grams huffs.

I chuckle while Griff and Ari smirk at the pair. This is typical behavior for my grandparents, and I don't know how their marriage survived fifty-plus years, but it has.

When the meals are delivered, the grandparents are too busy enjoying the food to argue. The pork tenderloin is the best I've ever had. This dinner is such a treat in so many ways. The companionship . . . The food . . . Even Grams' and Gramps' arguments. A ping of sadness hits that I won't be able to see these people every day.

Even though the girls declare we can't eat another bite, Gramps orders dessert. The waiter brings out chocolate lava cake and we pass it around, everyone taking a small bite. Both men give some good-natured ribbing to the women for all of us doing an about-face regarding the dessert.

I'm about ready to call it a night because I've got to start my drive across the country early tomorrow morning, but a tall handsome man winds his way towards us and catches my eye. His suit fits him like a glove, and there's a look of determination in his eyes.

My heart stops.

"I'll take it from here," Brent says in a gravelly voice once he's standing beside our table.

No one looks surprised to see him except for me; my mouth hangs open and I've lost the ability to form words.

Gramps stands and claps Brent on the back, then says, "Don't screw this up, son." The rest of the table occupants rise. Griff shakes Brent's hand, Ari gives him a jaunty wave, Grams hugs him, and Maggie does the "I'm watching you" gesture, two V-sign fingers brandished menacingly.

The newcomer smiles and nods, and the table clears out in ten seconds flat. I don't even have a chance to protest their departure. Brent takes a seat right beside me, pinning me with his gaze. "You look gorgeous in that dress. I'm so sorry that I missed it the first time."

My eyes widen. "How did you know this is the prom dress?"

"Grams and Griff might have mentioned you'd be wearing it. In fact, Griff was quite emphatic that I shouldn't miss this opportunity."

I cross my arms over my chest, realizing that my meddlesome family played a part in this unexpected meeting. "What are you doing here?" I say in a chilly tone.

His smile falters at my unfriendly greeting and he shifts in his chair. "I wanted to tell you something before you leave. I should have said this weeks ago."

My heart does several flips in my chest while my brain reminds me that he doesn't want me. *He only wants the team.*

"Libby, I'd regret it for the rest of my life if I let you go before telling you that I love you." I open my mouth to refute his words—citing the fake dating scheme—but he holds up a placating hand. "Please let me finish, then you can have your say."

I nod and clamp my lips together to keep the emotional tirade I want to spew out at his too-handsome face at bay.

"Even before you came to work for me, I knew I was in trouble of falling for you for real. You've always been the girl for me, but we've both been too stubborn and thickheaded to admit it."

He takes both my hands in his. "It wasn't a fake date for me when we went to the charity auction, and it wasn't fake when we went to the family reunion. The lunch hour debates were the most fun I'd had at work in years. But I wasn't sure how you felt, and I was too afraid to ask. Everything seemed to spiral out of control. You thought that all I wanted was the team, when in fact, all I wanted is you."

Our eyes connect and he reaches up and gently wipes the moisture off my cheeks with his thumbs. I didn't even realize that I was crying.

"Why didn't you say anything when I asked you if there was a reason for me to stay?" I choke out over the lump in my throat.

"I didn't want to be the reason you turn down your dream job, Libby. I still don't want to be."

I blow out a loud breath. "Then why are you here?"

He smiles. "Dad is going to sell the team."

I almost jump out of my chair. "What?! But why? What about the fake dating to convince him?" I stammer.

Brent squeezes my hand. "I realized that I didn't want or need all the stress—that impacted Dad's health and is now impacting mine. And I realized that a change of venue would be good for me."

My brows draw together. "A change of venue?" I repeat.

"There's a floundering minor league team just outside Boston that's for sale. Dad and I are going to buy it, and I'm going to turn that organization around." He gives me a flirty grin. "I might know an assistant curator who lives nearby. Maybe she'll agree to give me a chance. Start slow by going on a few real dates, then see where the relationship goes from there."

A sob escapes and I place my hand over my mouth. Tears are now falling down my face in earnest. "Do you mean it?" I whisper.

"Yes, with all my heart. I love you, Libby, and I'm going to prove it to you. Hopefully you'll admit that you love me too. Someday."

Someday is today, but I don't tell him that. I crossed the fine line between love and hate a long time ago.

"When are you moving?" I ask.

"Once the team is sold—hopefully that won't take long because Dad's put out feelers and already has a lot of interest.

Then I thought I'd find a place not too far from Cambridge. Close enough to work but not too far from the girl I want to woo."

I giggle. "Woo? You sound like Gramps."

Brent chuckles, then a worried expression crosses his face. "Are you in, Libby? Or should I just stay here and regret I lost you?"

Wanting him to grovel a little bit, I say with a steely stare, "Seems like this occasion warrants a grand gesture. Where's the ice cream?"

He looks around the room with a panicked expression on his face. Since there's no waiter in the vicinity, I back off my request, and lean over and whisper, "How about we seal it with a kiss instead?"

He tilts his head closer and kisses me, leaving no doubt in my mind that he means every word.

Epilogue – Love You Forever

Brent

Two Months Later

Children's voices and laughter float down the hall. My girlfriend is teaching an American history class to a group of six-year-olds today.

This should be interesting.

I hover at the door to watch. Libby is a natural, fielding all their questions while trying to teach them a little history. The group is like a rambunctious litter of puppies—they can't sit still. One small boy escapes from the pack, but Libby's assistant gently steers him back.

"Why did they wear those funny clothes?" a small girl asks when Libby shows them the Colonial-era clothing display.

"How did they go to the bathroom?" a boy asks staring intently at the breeches.

"Did they eat hamburgers? I like McDonalds," a cute sprite says.

Libby and I exchange grins. We both love kids and hopefully we'll have some someday. But I've got to get through today first. A little moisture breaks out on my palms.

Don't put the cart before the horse, Grandma would say.

After the class ends, the kids disperse with parents or caregivers. Their high-pitched voices chat animatedly about the history lesson. The one child is still asking about how colonists went to the bathroom. It was smart of Libby to leave that question to the parents—let them describe the ins and outs of an outhouse and pants with no zipper.

Libby gives me a kiss on the cheek and says, "I just need to get my stuff and I'm ready."

I nod. We're going to a fancy restaurant in Boston, but Libby doesn't know that. She thinks we're having hamburgers at a place we found that serves burgers that are almost as good as Wally's. *Almost.*

Once I drive away from Cambridge, her brows draw together. "I thought we were going to The Corner Burger Shack?"

"A slight change of plans," I say.

She gives me a narrow-eyed look. "Am I dressed okay?"

Her outfit is lovely, even though it's what she wears to work on most days. The sapphire blue button-down is a great color on her, and I love the way the black pants outline her figure.

"You look beautiful in everything, Libby."

She giggles. "Well, you're biased," she says. "Tell me about your day."

"Remember the star pitcher I'm trying to sign?"

She nods.

"I met with him and his agent this morning. Guess what I served them?"

"Some fancy pastries?"

I laugh. "Nope. I took a page from your playbook and bought some coffee and crullers at a local bakery. Thought I'd ply them with sugar and caffeine like when we signed Sam Hudson to his contract extension."

Libby smiles. "Well, did it work?"

"Nope. Remember the lunch fiasco with Dusty Sherman and his agent? When they turned their noses up at the very expensive, gourmet food?"

She grimaces. "Yes, I remember that only too well."

Poor Libby had busted her butt to bring in that meal and they wouldn't eat a bite. *Did I ever thank her properly for doing that?* Something to consider later. "The kid thinks he's God's gift to baseball. He and his agent turned their noses up at the 'commonplace crullers'—that's what the kid called them."

"Ouch. They insulted them to your face?" Libby replies with indignation in her voice.

"They did, but it was for the best. After they left, I felt defeated. Then something surprising happened."

Libby sits up straighter in her seat. "What?"

I grin remembering the irony of what happened next. "The twenty-something kid who's our equipment manager strolls in. He sees the crullers and asks if he can have one. I figure why not. We sat down and shared coffee and crullers for about an hour."

Libby arches an eyebrow. "That's surprising? Most people, aside from that snotty pitcher, don't turn down crullers."

I laugh. "That wasn't the surprising part. Turns out the kid was a star pitcher in high school, he even led his team to a state title. He didn't get any scholarship offers because his town is small, like really small. No college with a decent size baseball program gave him a chance."

Libby frowns. "That's a shame."

I nod. "He couldn't afford to go to college, so he's been working for the team ever since, hoping to get a chance to try out. He's going to try out next week. The kid is a gem, nicest guy you ever met. I sure hope he can pitch."

We both laugh.

When we pull up at the trendy seafood restaurant, the parking lot is packed. Libby's jaw drops open. "How did you get a reservation here?" she asks in awe.

"I know a guy," I say with a playful grin. It helps that the former owner of the minor league team I manage owns this place.

Once we're inside, the ambiance surrounds you like a comfortable glove. The place is rustic and looks like an old ship, complete with exposed wood beams on the ceiling and fishing paraphernalia—like nets, life vests, and even an old-fashioned ship's wheel—hanging on the walls. Every table is filled, and we have to wait a few minutes to be seated.

"It smells yummy," Libby comments as she reads the menu while we wait. I want to lean over and kiss her, but I don't. Just having her tucked by my side makes me feel like the luckiest man in the world.

After we're seated, my palms start to sweat again. I haven't been this nervous since prom when I sweated through my fancy shirt almost as soon as I put it on. I'm not sure I can eat a bite until I get this over with.

"Are you okay?" Libby asks once we've placed our orders. "You seem kind of fidgety."

I was going to wait and do this over ice cream, but instead I decide that I need to get this done before I sweat through my shirt. I fumble in my pocket but manage to retrieve the small object. My hands shake as I hold out the ring to Libby. "Libby, will you marry me?" I blurt, my prepared speech forgotten in my haste and nervousness.

Her eyes go round, and I wonder if I've jumped the gun. I promised we'd date for a while before doing this, but I just can't wait any longer. After what feels like minutes but is probably only seconds, she smiles and holds out her hand. I slip the ring on her finger, glad that I didn't drop it under the table or in the water carafe.

She gazes at her hand, a beaming smile on her face.

"I think I need a verbal answer," I say teasingly.

Her eyes fly to mine. "Yes! I'll marry you, Brent."

My body sags with relief.

"I think I've loved you since high school," she adds.

Her confession shocks me to the core. After The Debacle, I thought she hated me. "You have? Why didn't you tell me sooner?"

"The fake dating threw me off. I was scared to tell you. Then when you followed me here, I wanted you to be the one to make the move." She stares back down at the ring. "This is perfect," she whispers.

"Libby, can we forget about the fake dating? That's not something I'm very proud of."

She blinks back tears, the action doing strange things to my heart. I'm going to need a lifetime to make things right and convince her that I love her for real. I plow on, her silence making me start to panic. "I've loved you since high school as well. If I wasn't such an idiot, I would have proposed sooner. Please believe me when I say that I love you with all my heart."

Her eyes lock with mine. When she taps her heart with her hand and points at me, the gesture makes my heart soar. "We were both idiots, Brent. Maybe we were supposed to have a rocky path to each other, and it means our marriage will be smooth sailing."

Remembering all the ups and downs our relationship has gone through, I wonder whether our marriage can be smooth sailing. But I'm in for the long haul, even if we have a few bumps.

"Let's tell each other how we feel every single day. I don't want any doubts between us." I say.

"Okay," she says. "I'll start. I love you Mr. Bigshot."

I smirk. "I love you too, Soon-to-be Mrs. Bigshot."

"Just think how happy Fred and Wilma will be, seeing each other every day," Libby adds with a flirty wink.

Rolling my eyes, I say, "Is that the reason you said yes?"

Libby's smile lights up the room. "I may have a crush on Fred's owner," she teases. Her eyes widen and she claps her hands. "Do you think your mom still has those dates in October reserved at the Wilshire Gardens?" she asks. "That's the perfect place for a wedding, especially if we have canine ring bearers."

I blink. She wants to include Fred and Wilma in the wedding? I'm certainly not going to stand in the way especially since we reconnected at the dog park. "Can you pull off a wedding in a month?"

She smiles. "Yes, I can! Maggie, Ari, and Grams will help. I'm sure your mom will be willing to pitch in as well."

I grab my phone and shoot off a text. Might as well find out right now whether the dates are still reserved. My phone pings a few seconds later. I laugh when I read the message, then turn the screen to Libby.

Mom: I've got October 10 and 17 reserved. What took you so long to ask?

I jump up, round the table, and plant a toe-curling kiss on Libby. "How does October 10 sound?"

She kisses me back then smiles. "Like the start of the best days of the rest of my life."

Mine too.

        THE END

Note to Readers

Dear Reader—thank you for reading Book 4 in my new Rom-Com series, **Too Busy for Love**—clean and wholesome romantic comedies filled with humor, quirky characters, and laugh-out-loud situations. As the saying goes, "laughter is the best medicine," and we can all use more laughter in our lives.

Libby's roommate Maggie and her boss star in the next book, ***Crushing on the Boss***. It will be a rocky ride with lots of laughs. I plan on publishing this book in fall 2023.

Are you a fan of my Connor Brothers series of sweet, small-town romance? I'm doing a spin off series, Connor Brothers Next Generation. Book 1, ***Always and Forever*** will be published in summer 2023. Watch my newsletter for all future book announcements.

An author's most gratifying reward for all our hard work is that you enjoy one of our books and find inspiration in the story. Let me know it that's the case! I love hearing from my readers—Email me at leahb1959@gmail.com. Also, please take a moment to leave a review on Amazon. Just a few words can inspire another reader to take a chance on this book.

Please follow me on my website, Facebook, or Amazon author page or subscribe to my newsletter to be informed about upcoming book releases. Links to all of those are included in the "About the Author" chapter below.

Thank You and Happy Reading.

Acknowledgements

Thank you to my amazing editor Bonnie McKnight. She's been with me every step of the way, including on this new series. Her suggestions and encouraging comments improved this story. She makes me a better writer and I truly appreciate her wisdom and guidance.

I'm thankful for all the wonderful people in my life. A little piece of each of you finds its way into my stories. And I'm especially grateful to my supportive husband who chuckles when he sees himself in one of my books.

About the Author

Leah Busboom wanted to become an author since the day she learned how to read. She specializes in the Romance genre because she loves sweet romances with a happy ending. Her books are known for their heartwarming stories, intriguing characters, and hilarious real-life situations that will make you want to laugh out loud.

Leah currently lives in Colorado with her wonderful husband, her "Blue Bomber" bicycle and a hundred bunny rabbits that roam free in the neighborhood.

Find out about Leah's latest book releases, sales, and giveaways.

- AuthorLeahBusboom.com
- Newsletter Sign-up
- Leah Busboom Facebook Author Page
- Amazon Author Page

Books by Leah Busboom: (all available on Amazon)

My hilarious new Rom-Com series has the perfect blend of laugh-out-loud scenes and heart-touching moments.

Too Busy for Love series: (Clean, laugh-out-loud Rom-Coms):

- *Shopping for the Grump* – Avery & Gavin's story (Book 1)
- *Cooking for the CEO* – Ash & Teddy's story (Book 2)
- *Planning for the All-*Star — Ari and Griff's story (Book 3)
- *Fake Dating the Grumpy Bigshot* – Libby and Brent's story (Book 4)

Paradise Springs series: (Clean Christian romance with humor & heart)

If you loved my Potter's House (Three) Christian romance books, my Paradise Springs series is a spin-off of those books, featuring your favorite characters, plus introducing new ones.

- *The Melody of Joy* – Juanita and Brenden's story (Book 1)
- *The Song of Grace* – Amber and Mack's story (Book 2)
- *The Music of Love* – Marci and Jared's story (Book 3)
- *The Chorus of Happiness* – Christine and Reid's story (Book 4)

The Potter's House (Three) series: (Clean Christian romance - Stories of hope, redemption, and second chances)

- *A Time for Faith* – Rae & Noah's story (Book 6)
- *A Reason for Hope* – Riley & Logan's story (Book 13)
- *The Courage for Love* – Ellie & Zander's story (Book 20)
- Potter's House Series Box Set – All three books in a box set collection

Love at Christmas Inn series: (Holiday Christian romance)

- *Snow Angel* – Willow & Jace's story
- *Cupcake Angel* – Harper & Chase's story
- *Glitter Angel* — Lexi and Brady's story

Connor Brothers Series: (Clean & Wholesome small-town romance)

Here's the complete series so far:

- *Finding You*—Hailey and Quinn's story (Book 1)

- *Loving You*—Maddie and Max's story (Book 2)
- *Wanting You*—Daisy and Jacob's story (Book 3)
- *Needing You*—Ashleigh and Brock's story (Book 4)
- *Mistletoe, Tinsel & You*—Sylvie and Ford's story (A Holiday Rom-Com, Book 5)
- *Casseroles, Kisses & You*—Bea and Nate's story (A Sweet Rom-Com, Book 6)
- *Rescue Me*—Starr and Bryce's story (Book 7)
- *Inspire Me*—Addison and Ian's story (Book 8)
- *Choose Me*—Luci and Austin's story (Book 9)
- *Return to Me* – Mary Sue and Cooper's story (Book 10)
- *The Holly Berry Dress & You* – Amelia and Doug's story (A Geeky Rom-Com, Book 11)
- *Forever You* – Laci, Matthew, and Jeremy's story (Book 12) (2022 International Readers' Favorite bronze medal winner). Also available in Audiobook.
- *Connor Brothers Box Set* — Books 1–4 in the series

Coming Soon! Connor Brothers Next Generation (Clean & Wholesome small-town romance featuring the Connor Brothers kids)

- *Always and Forever* – Lilly and Noah's story (Book 1)

Chance on Love Series Trilogy:

Note: These books are steamier than my other series. They contain mild, on-page intimacy.

- *Second Chances*—Matt and Samantha's story (Book 1)

- *Taking Chances*—Danny and Paige's story (Book 2) (Winner: 2018 Rocky Mountain Cover Art Contest—Sweetest Cover)
- *Lasting Chances*—Gabe and Megan's story (Book 3)
- Chance on Love Series Boxed Set – Books 1–3 in Chance on Love series

Unlikely Catches Series Trilogy:

Note: These books are steamier than my other series. They contain mild, on-page intimacy.

- *Catching Cash's Heart*—Holly and Cash's story (Angel Wings & Fastballs) (Book 1)
- *Stealing Alan's Heart*—Brianna and Alan's story (Stilettos & Spreadsheets) (Book 2)
- *Winning Trey's Heart*—Abby and Trey's story (Playboy & the Bookworm) (Book 3)
- *Unwrapping Sam's Heart* – Lynn and Sam's story (A Christmas Novella) (Prequel to Book
- *Melting Nick's Heart* – Bethany and Nick's story (A Valentine's Day Novella) (Sequel to Book 3)